RESORT
TO
MURDER

RESORT
TO
MURDER

•

Mary Ellen Hughes

AVALON BOOKS
NEW YORK

PRINTED IN THE UNITED STATES OF AMERICA
ON ACID-FREE PAPER
BY HADDON CRAFTSMEN, BLOOMSBURG, PENNSYLVANIA

For Terry, with love

Chapter One

July 22, 1974

Merle pulled into the parking lot of the brightly lit diner, tires crunching gravel, and turned off the ignition. The car shuddered to a stop. Got to get that fixed sometime, he thought. A neon sign in the window blinked at him, hypnotically whispering "Alma's" over and over, and promising "good food." He looked over at his young passenger, a kid he had picked up a couple hours ago in West Virginia. A boy, barely nineteen, who needed a ride to Maryland, looking for the job he couldn't find back home.

"Well, kid, this is where we part ways. You should be able to catch another ride easy here. C'mon in and I'll buy you a cup of coffee."

They pushed through the door and eased onto two stools in front of the near-empty counter. The aroma of freshly made coffee and doughnuts filled the air, and Karen Carpenter's mellow voice crooned through the radio. A young,

1

heavy set waitress in a blue and white checked uniform came up to them, pulling a pencil from her hair, ready to take their order.

"Two coffees."

She nodded, then pulled up crockery and spoons from a lower shelf, setting them down with a soft clatter. As she poured from a glass coffee pot, the music changed to news, and a brisk male voice reported the latest developments in the Patty Hearst kidnapping case. She had been identified as one of a group of bank robbers, members of the SLA.

"Ain't that something?" the man asked. "A girl as rich as her, gettin' into all that. Looks like that kidnapping thing was one big joke on everybody."

The waitress barely raised her eyes from what she was doing. "Mmm," she said. She put the pot back on the burner and began to turn away.

"Hey," he said. "I remember you. From Madison High. Class of '63." He struggled to think of her name, and gave up. "Remember me? Merle Haisler?"

The young woman's eyes widened, then showed recognition. "Yeah, sure. How're you doing, Merle?"

"Doin' pretty good. Got me a job as district salesman, for Hirsch and Eland. You got a tractor? I'll sell you some parts for it."

The woman grinned. "That's great, Merle."

"So what's new with you?"

"Oh, nothing much." She glanced over her shoulder, as though there was something she had to do.

"You hear from any of the old group?" he asked. "Go to reunions or anything?" As he said it, he remembered she hadn't been part of his old group, or part of any group, for that matter. She had been a quiet loner—nice enough, he supposed, but not someone he ever spent more than a fleeting thought on.

She shook her head.

"Yeah, me neither. But I read about what happened to

Jim and Cherilynn, about their baby, you know? Who woulda thought somethin' like that could happen back there? I mean, it's not like they're rich or anything. I might go see them when I'm in town," Merle said, aware of a stiffening in the woman as she stood before him, thinking she must feel as bad for them as he did. "But, heck, what do you say? I mean, they got another kid, but still. . . ."

An older woman with blond hair piled high came up and nudged the waitress. "You got a call," she said, her voice kept low. "Your babysitter again. You gotta do something about all these calls, you know. Alma's gettin' sick of it."

"Hey, you got a kid?" Merle asked.

The waitress just looked at him, then turned and hurried into the kitchen.

Merle watched her, noticing for the first time the thin gold band on her left hand. He turned to the teen next to him. "It's a small world, kid. Who'd a thought I'd run into someone like her after more'n ten years. And who'd a guessed that she . . . well, it just shows you never know." He shrugged and sipped his coffee, which wasn't bad at all. He'd had worse, with all the places he had to drive through.

He looked up as she suddenly reappeared, holding two plates of chocolate cream pie that she set down in front of them.

"On the house for an old school buddy," she said, with a wide, pleased smile.

The boy's face lit up as he reached for his. Merle realized the kid must have been hungry and felt a twinge of guilt for not asking him. He grinned at her though, and said, "Well, ain't that nice. Thanks, hon."

"And I put extra whipped cream on yours, Merle," she said. "I remember you liked that."

Merle nodded, wondering how in hell she happened to remember that, and dug into the pie. The boy was easing the cream off his, and Merle reached over with his fork and scooped it up. "No use wasting it," he said, laughing. She waited a few moments, said "Enjoy," then moved down the counter to wait on a new customer.

Merle finished his pie and sat for a while, smoking a cigarette, chatting with the boy and people nearby about the weather, the latest game. Finally he drained his cup and pushed it away from him.

"Well, I gotta get on the road." He stood up, hiking up his pants, tucking in his shirt. He stifled a yawn. "Nice seein' you, hon," he called to the waitress. What the heck was her name? "And thanks again." He turned to the boy, pulled a ten out of his pocket, and slid it over to him. "Good luck, kid."

As he climbed into his car, Merle thought about the boy. Just nineteen, and scrambling for work. It's a tough life sometimes. Merle felt lucky to have his steady job, a job with a future, he hoped, but at least a job with a regular paycheck. Things weren't too bad. With what Jeanine was making, maybe they could afford. . . . He yawned again. Better get on to Fredrick, find a cheap room quick, and get some sleep.

He pulled onto Route 70 and eased into traffic. Not too busy this time of night. The headlights in his rearview mirror bothered his eyes, though. He looked away, rubbed at them. Yeah, maybe they could start looking at houses, small ones. His eyes still felt raw, kinda blurry. Should he pull over? Nah, he wasn't that tired. Shouldn't be. He just had coffee. He'd perk up in a minute. The radio. He needed something to listen to.

Merle reached for the radio knob. A horn blared. What the heck! Had he wandered to the next lane? Better concentrate. Blurry. Things looked blurry. He blinked, tried to clear it away. Eyes heavy. So heavy. He opened his window to get a little cool air on his face.

Take some deep breaths. Wake up. Tired. So damn tired.

What's that up there? That big shape. Can't see. A truck? It doesn't have its lights on. It's not moving. My God. It's parked on the shoulder and *I'm* on the shoulder! Pull out! Pull out! Too late! No!

Chapter Two

June 18, 1999

LeAnn Rimes' song on the small portable radio ended, and the news reporter began talking about the latest backup on the outer loop of the Baltimore beltway. Maggie reached for the off button but stopped in dismay as she saw her red, wet fingertips.

"You'll have to hurry, Maggie!" Agnes called from the doorway.

"I know, I know," Maggie answered, grabbing for a wad of tissues, the exasperation in her voice aimed as much at her inky fingers as at the school secretary. Maggie grumbled about cheap, leaky pens.

"Mr. Braun wants those grades in by noon, dear. He wants to be out of here and on his way to Ocean City."

Maggie held in the irritation she felt, as she had often controlled it when dealing with Agnes during the last three years—Maggie's entire teaching career to date. The woman was a relentless nagger on behalf of her boss, Principal Braun. She obviously thought it was more important to get her esteemed boss on his way to the beach on time than to have carefully calculated grades. Or possibly Agnes thought grades were produced by wiggling one's nose?

"He'll have them," Maggie said with a tight smile, "just as soon as I've done them."

Agnes' pale, wrinkled face puckered with disapproval. "Well, I certainly hope that will be by noon," she said. She jerked her head out the doorway and clicked her stubby heels down the hall, searching, Maggie was sure, for other recalcitrant teachers to badger.

Maggie threw the red-stained wad of tissues into the wastebasket and grumbled aloud about unreasonable deadlines, certain high school principals, and the school system in general. Since she was alone, she felt free to vent her opinions freely, although Mac, her office mate, had suffered through some of her complaints in the past. She could pretty well guess how he would have commented if he were there, with his dry wit given to quotations from his beloved field of English literature.

Just the other day, after Maggie had spent hours grading geometry exams and felt more than a little exasperated with the faulty logic of a few of her students, she had leaned back in her chair and groaned. "Mac, I need a vacation. A change of scene to recharge my batteries. I'm feeling burned out."

Mac had looked over in his heavy-lidded way from his side of the room and replied, "Get thee to a nunnery, Maggie."

"I'd love to," she said. "As soon as I find a nice, peaceful one. Do cloistered convents have tennis courts?"

It was then that he told her about the Highview, a mountain resort somewhere in western Maryland. He and his wife, Ali, had spent a pleasant weekend there a couple years ago, he said. He even located a phone number for her, printed on one of the many cards tucked into his bulging wallet. Mac was a saver, a fact evident by a glance at his messy half of the office.

Maggie wrote it down, called immediately, and promptly made a reservation. Now there was a room waiting for her, and she would be heading for it as soon as she had finished grading. Carefully. At her own pace. And to her own satisfaction. If she could only find a pen that didn't leak.

Chapter Three

Lori felt the hot June sun bring prickles of sweat to her face as she moved quickly over the grass, away from the Highview's kitchen. She wiped at the moisture and turned to look back at the side door she had had to prop open because of its automatic lock. She saw a flash of sunlight, a reflection off the metal trim of the door. The brick must have slipped, she thought. Or did someone move the door?

She shook off the thought and glanced at her watch. No one saw her leave, she was sure. And there was time. They shouldn't miss her for a few minutes, and she would be back before the lunch rush. She picked up her pace as she came closer to the cool shade of the trees ahead, clutching the book in her hand.

Lori stepped carefully onto the mulched path with the white sneakers that formed part of her summer waitress uniform. "*Clean* white sneakers," the manager, Ms. Crawford, had warned her that first day of work, so she watched where she set them on the path that wound through the

9

trees. After a few minutes she was deep into the woods. She slowed down and looked around. Now where . . . ?

"Lori! Over here!"

Lori spun around and smiled.

"Oh, there you are." She walked to the small clearing and ducked under a low-hanging poplar branch, her pony-tail brushing against the bark. "I was afraid. . . . It's getting late. I'll have to hurry."

Lori didn't see the rock as it came crashing onto her skull. She didn't feel the blood seep through her light brown hair, and she never heard the words spoken above her limp and lifeless body.

"No hurry."

Chapter Four

It was two P.M. when Maggie finally took off in her '95 burgundy Dodge Shadow, the red ink scrubbed off her fingers. Agnes's relentless urgings to hurry had only made her tense, but gradually, as the miles ticked by, she felt the pressures of the last few days slip away—all, that is, except one big one.

"Maggie, you're not coming with us to Bethany Beach?" Her mother's shocked, hurt voice still sounded in her head.

"Mom, I've gone with all of you to Bethany for every summer of my life. I want to do something on my own for a change."

Maggie still saw her mother's face, non-understanding, *mis*understanding. The family had always vacationed together, including grandparents, aunts and uncles, and cousins. They had loved it as kids, hadn't they, she and her brother, Joe? Why should that stop? What was wrong?

What was wrong was Maggie now felt smothered by it all, but she couldn't tell her mother that. Or her dad. She

knew he was hurt too, and neither of them would understand, which added to her frustration. But at least Joe would
go, her easygoing, younger brother, Joe, in graduate school
now and perfectly content to come and go as the family
dictated on his days off.

Part of the problem was that Maggie had exactly one
week of free time. She had signed up to work at a summer
math camp for middle-school kids. It ran in three-week
segments, beginning a week after school, and she would be
working up to the start of the next school year.

She would have loved to be able to take the whole summer off, but she needed the money to finish paying off
lingering college debts. So this was her only time to relax:
seven days to do exactly what *she* wanted to do, for a
change. And she didn't particularly want to spend it tagging
along after relatives at the beach like a twelve-year-old,
listening to the same old stories that came up over and over.
She loved her family, of course, and she always would. But
they would just have to face it. She had grown up.

Maggie frowned at the road ahead of her, her muscles
tight, and she realized this was no way to start a vacation.
She shook off all the negative thoughts that had been causing her tension and switched from replay to fast forward.
She thought of the Highview, and wondered what it would
be like.

She was excited about going there, but an uneasy worry
crept in. Maybe she had made a mistake, rushing with her
plans. Besides, what did Mac and Ali consider a pleasant
getaway place, anyway? It wasn't as if she knew them all
that well. For all she knew they might be weekend nudists.
At the thought of this Maggie laughed out loud.

She toyed with the idea that the Highview might be a
sunny, mountain nudist resort. She then tried to picture her
dignified co-worker at a nudist colony, but her mind kept
wrapping a modest sheet around his portly shape, toga-

style, and he spouted verses from *Julius Caesar* to his equally modest wife as they lounged beside a pool.

Maggie reached for a sourball from a small bag on the passenger seat, unwrapped it, and popped it into her mouth. Tangy Cherry. Well, she knew some things about the place. It had a pool. And tennis courts. And judging from the name, a great view, which was all she required for now. Having checked the map carefully before taking off, she knew too that it wasn't far from the Civil War battlefield of Antietam, and the farmhouse where John Brown had stayed as he planned his raid on nearby Harper's Ferry, West Virginia. If the Highview got too quiet, she could always sightsee.

Small towns whizzed by, and she began to amuse herself with math games to pass the time. Let's see, if I left Baltimore at one o'clock, driving up Route 70 at 50 miles an hour. . . . No, let's make it harder, 47 miles an hour, and someone left Hagerstown, Maryland, which is what—60 miles away?—at one forty-five, driving at 42 miles an hour, where would we meet and at what time?

She grinned as she recalled groans from the rest of the class when this kind of question came up in what—fifth grade? sixth? But she'd always loved it, because she could come up with the answer, eventually, with a little scribbling with pencil and paper. And now she could do it in her head, while driving, to pass the time. Well, some people can sing, or paint pictures. She happened to be good with numbers. To each his/her own. She continued her mental calculating.

She exited Interstate 70 West and took the smaller and narrower roads that wound their way high into the mountains. Towns gave way to farmland, and fields of corn or soybeans gave way to dense forests. Soon she found herself skirting a sharply rising slope up a mountain, with a guardrail on the opposite side edging a steep drop while the road took several sharp turns. Maggie slowed to a comfortable speed, grateful that no one was behind her, and watched carefully for a sign that said Highview.

Ah, there it was—a large, white-painted board, weather-beaten enough to have been there from the Civil War itself. Maggie turned and heard the crunch of her tires on a white, graveled driveway.

The driveway wound its own twisted way through dense trees, and Maggie had to watch the road so closely that she was startled when the trees suddenly ended. Before her stood the Highview. She took a deep breath and smiled.

The Highview Inn was a beautiful, modern lodge-hotel tucked into the side of the mountain. A blending of stone and natural-finish wood, together with large windows that reflected the world outside, made it a part of its environment. Maggie also noted the understated landscaping as she drove up to the entrance. It was attractive but unobtrusive, almost as if the plants and shrubs growing there had sprung up from seeds that had dropped naturally in particularly convenient and pleasing spots. It was a vision of peace and tranquility—just what she wanted.

She laughed when she spotted two guests strolling on the grounds. They were clothed, not in togas, but in comfortable shorts and T-shirts. And they looked very relaxed and contented, a condition Maggie hoped to reach as soon as possible.

She parked her car and allowed a college-aged boy from the Inn to help carry her bags into the lobby. As she waited at the desk to be checked in, she did her own checking out of the scene. Not bad, she thought, feeling her smile grow as her eyes panned the spacious lounge area. Plump tan sofas and chairs dotted it, several facing large windows that looked out onto green lawns and a blue, sparkling pool. Maggie mentally plopped herself down on one of the couches, kicked off her shoes, and sighed with satisfaction.

The silver-haired man in a navy blazer who had been processing the necessary paperwork behind the desk interrupted her reverie. "You play?" he asked with a smile, inclining his head toward the tennis racquet handle protruding from one of the bags at her feet.

"I try," Maggie said.

"I asked that somewhat obvious question because we keep daily lists of guests looking for tennis partners. Another young lady called just a few minutes ago. She would like to play this afternoon at four. Would you be interested?"

"Sure, as long as she's not a second Martina Hingis."

"No, no," he said. "Nothing like that. The young lady in question is Dyna Hall. She specifically asked for someone who, and I quote, 'didn't mind chasing moon-balls.' "

"Sounds just about my speed. Four o'clock, you said?"

"Yes, Miss Olenski. Or do you prefer Ms.?" He drew out his *z-z-z*'s with a smile curving up the ends of his mouth.

"Maggie's fine. Thanks" —she looked at the nametag on his lapel—"Charles."

Maggie picked up her key and raised it to him in farewell, then followed the bellboy to the elevator. She was just about to step on when Charles called to her, waving a small piece of paper.

"I just realized you have a message here," he said.

Maggie trotted back, puzzled, and took it. Her brow puckered in annoyance as she scanned it. It was from her mother, wanting her to call to let her know she had arrived safely. Maggie shoved it in her pocket and resolved to wait before responding. She would be able to handle it better after she had wound down a little. But as she got back on the elevator and watched the bellboy punch her floor button, a small guilt feeling crept in, which annoyed her even more.

Forty-five minutes later, unpacked and wearing white cotton shorts and a green T-shirt, Maggie followed the signs to the tennis courts. She crossed the sunny expanse of lawn that stretched away from the pool area, then stepped onto a mulched pathway that became a cooler, sun-dappled passageway through the wooded area, with thick, leafy branches touching overhead. She took deep breaths of the sweet, woodsy fragrance as she walked. It took only a few steps to lose sight of both pool and hotel, and to see nothing ahead but plant life.

A lifelong city-dweller, Maggie was suddenly trans-ported to another world, one much darker and quieter than any backyard garden or city park she had ever been in. The unfamiliarity began to make her uneasy. Her steps slowed, and she started looking more closely at the terrain as she went. What was that on the path up there? A snake! No, just a twisty dead branch. She began to wish she weren't quite so alone. How far were those courts?

The temperature was at least ten degrees cooler than it had been out in the sun, and Maggie rubbed her bare upper arms, shifting racquet and tennis balls. A branch brushed her leg and made her jump. She laughed nervously at her-self. Maggie walked on for what seemed too long a time, then turned a sharp corner in the pathway. She drew a quick breath. There, up ahead, finally, were the courts.

"Should have warned me to wear my hiking boots," she muttered. "It wouldn't surprise me if I saw a moose grazing over by one of the courts."

As she got closer, she noticed a very un-mooselike crea-ture watching her. He was tall, dark, and had much better legs than any moose she had seen. Judging from his Highview-labeled shirt and shorts, she guessed he was the tennis pro.

"Hi," he said as she drew closer, and as if all his other attributes weren't enough, long, masculine dimples ap-peared as he smiled. "Need any help?"

Taking a deep, calming breath, Maggie said, "No, not now that I've actually found this place. But I was beginning to wonder if these courts were somewhere in West Virginia."

The dimples grew deeper as a chuckle rolled out. "I know what you mean," he said. "I think they must have searched hard for the most level spot they could find. A lot of people complain about the extra time it takes to get here. You need a court?"

"I'm supposed to meet Dyna Hall for a match. I assumed she reserved one."

"Let's take a look." He led Maggie into the sports shop, a low, red brick building nearby, and checked the sign-up sheets spread out on a counter. "Dyna Hall. . . ." He ran his left hand down the list, and Maggie noticed it was ringless. "Yup! Here she is. Court five. She's signed in and should be over there now."

"Thanks," Maggie said, then turned to leave.

"Hold on, your name is . . . ?" He grabbed a pencil and held it poised.

"Maggie Olenski. O-l-e-n-s-k-i."

He wrote her name then smiled at her. "Hi, Maggie. I'm Rob Clayton. Resident tennis pro. If you need any lessons, I'm the one to call." He flashed her a set of straight, white teeth and gave her a look that lasted a fraction of a second too long. Maggie was annoyed to find herself becoming flustered. She pretended a sudden, overwhelming interest in a nearby rack of warm-up suits to hide her reaction.

"Well, we'll see how I do today," she said, as she examined a silky sleeve.

You've been cloistered in the classroom for too long, she chided herself, when she finally managed to walk away from the building. One slightly attractive male smiles at you and you react like a fourteen-year-old. But there was something about his easy flirtation that bothered her too. Maybe it seemed just a little too practiced?

She shrugged off the thought and watched the activity on the courts as she walked along the outside of a high, green fence. A couple of mixed doubles games were in progress on courts one and two, with two flushed and sweating middle-aged males resting on the sidelines of court three. A solitary woman worked on her serve on court four, reaching regularly into a tall orange basket filled with balls. Court five, as Maggie approached it, seemed at first glance to be empty.

Maggie looked around and finally saw a figure seated crosslegged near the net, her back against the fence. As Maggie approached she realized the young woman's eyes were closed.

"Are you all right?" Maggie asked, after some hesitation.

"Meditating."

"What?"

"Meditating."

"Oh. I'm sorry." Maggie stepped back, wondering what to do. She walked a few feet away and put her gear down, glancing back at the person she assumed to be Dyna Hall. She was blond, with a lot of thick, curly hair bunched and pinned in an odd arrangement. She wore purple sweats cut down to shorts and a sleeveless top. Maggie watched the woman on court four hit her serve into the net a few times, then looked back again at Dyna. She was just considering slipping quietly away when the woman's eyes snapped open.

"There," Dyna said, and jumped up, brushing off her backside.

Too late. Maggie smiled and walked over.

"You must be Maggie," the blond woman said. "Hi! I'm Dyna—with a 'Y.' Everyone gets it wrong, so don't worry. Sorry to make you wait, but I always try to meditate before I do anything challenging. It really helps. You ever try it?"

Maggie looked at her prospective opponent's open, friendly face and decided she'd probably like her, despite definite indications of oddness. She was about Maggie's age, possibly a year or two younger, with a pretty face and a sturdy figure. Her blond hair was many-shaded, going from light brown near the scalp to near white at the ends, and had a few streaks of orange here and there.

"Uh, no, I guess I never have," Maggie said, pulling her eyes away from the hair to answer.

Dyna-with-a-Y talked on about the value and methods of meditation, and leaned against the net post to stretch her leg muscles. Maggie pulled her racquet out of its cover and assumed an expression of polite attention, as she tried to remember the correct grip for a backhand volley. After trying a few, none of which felt particularly familiar, she decided she would probably just stay back near the baseline most of the time—forget the volleys. Dyna's dangling, crystal earrings flashed in the sun.

"OK! Shall we start?" Dyna was spinning her racquet, waiting for Maggie to call up or down. Maggie suddenly began to worry that maybe she was overmatched. Most of the games she had played before, the person with the most balls in her pockets simply walked back and started serving.

"Up?" she said, tentatively.

Dyna looked at the end of her racquet handle. "You got it."

Maggie soon found she needn't have worried. Her first serve, which dropped softly into the service court, was returned by Dyna into the net. The second was swung at and missed.

"Ace!" Dyna called, and Maggie laughed.

The match continued in that vein, with Maggie winning, mostly because she managed to keep from double-faulting and seemed to be the only one of the two who knew how to keep score. At one point, however, Dyna returned the ball quite a distance from Maggie, still keeping it inside the line. Maggie ran for it and swung wildly. The ball sailed high and disappeared over the fence and into the shrubbery.

"Out!" Dyna yelled, grinning. "Definitely out." She started to head for the gate.

"No, don't bother," Maggie called to her. "I hit it out. I'll get it later."

"Okay," Dyna said, and they played out the set, with Maggie winning it, six games to two. They walked to a shady spot near the fence and sat down, fanning their faces.

"Oof! I must be in rotten shape," Maggie said, breathing hard.

"It's the heat. And the altitude too. Less oxygen, you know."

"Are we that high up?"

"Doesn't take much." Dyna reached back and pulled her long hair off her neck with one hand, fanning it with the other. "The human body has to get acclimated, you know. Have you had your hemoglobin checked lately?"

"Uh, no."

Dyna launched on a rambling explanation of blood tests, then moved on to other areas of medicine. But Maggie, after recalling her companion's recent performance on the court, was beginning to feel her air of expertise on the subject was just that—mere air. She listened politely anyway, enjoying the ease and confidence with which Dyna tossed around medical terms.

After a while, when Dyna seemed to have run down, Maggie changed the subject to Rob Clayton.

"Who? Dimples?" Dyna asked. Maggie laughed and nodded. "He's a hunk, isn't he?" Dyna continued. "Pretty good pro, too. I heard he actually played at Wimbledon."

"Really?" Maggie said.

"I don't know how he ended up here, but they're lucky they've got him. I imagine he's quite a draw. In more ways than one."

Dyna told Maggie about a new racquet Rob had recommended that she was considering buying, but Maggie's attention began to wander. She was tired. It had been a full day. They probably should finish one more set then she'd head back to her room. Have a shower and relax before dinner.

A squirrel ran down a tree on the other side of the fence, stopped to look at them, and ran on. Maggie stood up and stretched.

"I'll go get that ball before I forget where I lobbed it," she said.

"Oh, right. I think it went over there." Dyna pointed.

Maggie squeezed through the rusty-hinged gate and walked along the fence, peering into the bushes. "How far back? Do you remember?"

"Not too far, I think. It might have rolled."

Maggie walked deeper into the wild undergrowth behind their court, her eyes searching the ground. She pulled branches aside and looked under them. What does poison ivy look like? she wondered, as she picked up a long stick to poke around with. Something white caught her eye. What's that? A shoe? Why would someone leave a——

"Dyna." The name caught in her throat as she struggled to scream it out. "Dyna!"

Maggie stood frozen, looking down at the body of the young woman lying in a small clearing, hair matted with dark, dried blood, her pale, lifeless skin mottled by dancing shadows.

"What is it?" Dyna called back.

"I need . . . help," Maggie cried. Her breath was coming faster as disjointed thoughts of CPR raced through her head, knowing at the same time that it would be useless. She looked again at the chalky skin below and wondered giddily what the girl's hemoglobin level could possibly be. She was almost on the point of a horrified giggle when Dyna ran up to her.

"What's the matt—oh, my God."

Chapter Five

"Help! Help! We need some help here." Dyna's voice rang down the courts. Maggie turned to see players stop in midplay, stare, then drop their racquets and move to respond. She turned back to look at the pitiful figure on the ground, looking now beyond the blood, and a new horror suddenly engulfed her as she did. Her hand flew to her mouth and she stepped back, knocking into Dyna.

"What? Are you all right? What's wrong?"

Maggie looked at Dyna, barely seeing her, then with an effort pulled herself together.

"I know her. Dyna, I *know* her!"

One of the two middle-aged men from court three arrived first, puffing and scrambling for the gate latch. The lone woman on court four hung back, and when she heard the man call back to his partner that there was a dead body here, let out a piercing scream. Others rushed over, and the area rapidly grew cluttered with noise and confusion as

22

people alternately held back, horrified, then pushed closer for a better look.

"Everybody please move back," Maggie insisted, shaking herself now to take charge, her teacher's tone of authority coming to her automatically. Her head swirled with conflicting thoughts and feelings, but as she had often found in the classroom, she could rise above that when necessary to keep a situation under control.

"This girl is dead. We have to call the police. You," she pointed to a woman from the mixed doubles foursome, a woman who looked fairly calm and competent, "run to the sports shop and call them." The woman nodded, grim-faced, and took off, and Maggie edged everyone back on the court and away from the dead girl.

The dead girl. Maggie looked back at her. Lori. It was Lori Basker. First row, third desk, second period geometry. Lori, whose eyes had squinted with the effort of understanding, whose soft brown hair had fallen over her face as she bent over a test paper. That hair was now plastered with blood over a crushed skull. Those eyes were glazed and unseeing. Maggie turned away. Lori had been murdered. The thought was almost incomprehensible.

"You okay?" Dyna looked at her with concern.

"I guess so."

Maggie heard a siren, far away. Before long the place would be filled with police, asking questions. What would she say? More people came. Maggie saw Rob Clayton running from the sports shop. She closed her eyes and hugged herself.

"C'mon. Let's go sit down over there, out of the way. Rob's here. He can take over now." Dyna tugged at her, and Maggie let herself be led to a quieter corner of the court. She had to think.

* * *

With the arrival of the police the tension for Maggie only increased as they rushed about, shouting orders, pushing people back, cordoning off the area. Maggie was pointed out, and a young deputy took her aside and asked questions over the noise, taking notes on when and how she had found the body. The young woman had been identified; she had been a waitress at the Highview.

Maggie told him how she knew Lori. He nodded and wrote it down. He asked about a book that had been found next to the body. She hadn't noticed it and could only say it wasn't hers, it must have been Lori's. Technicians took pictures of the crime scene, and measurements, and searched meticulously through the brush, obviously looking for evidence.

A second official came over to Maggie. He introduced himself as Sheriff Burger, a tall, heavy set man with thinning hair. He asked the same questions the first one had. She answered as clearly as she could, trying hard to control a tremor which had begun deep in her stomach. She knew it wasn't the sheriff giving her the shakes. It was the whole unbelievable scene that unnerved her.

After what seemed like hours they told Maggie she could go. What was wrong? Why didn't she want to go, leave this terrible scene? Bits and pieces of the things some of the deputies had said, talking to each other within earshot, ran through her head: "Blunt force, four or five hours ago, not much to go on, no weapon, sheriff's pretty busy, the perp's probably in Florida by now." The expressions on their faces were disinterested, and sometimes they actually laughed over comments to each other. It was their job, she knew that. They needed to be detached. But it bothered her.

She saw Rob Clayton moving about. There was nothing for him to do either, but he still hovered. She wondered why. Was he simply looking out for the hotel property which he managed, which was his responsibility? But his focus was constantly on the murder scene. Occasionally someone in a hotel uniform would come up to him, questioning. He answered brusquely, seeming impatient at the interruption, his eyes always on the police activity, and the questioner would move on.

Rob's intensity seemed curious. Maggie didn't see sadness or distress at the murder of a fellow employee, though, but a more detached, more intellectual determination simply to see everything, to know everything the police did.

Her head swiveled away from Rob when she heard a voice call the sheriff. "Mayor wants to talk to you," the deputy said. The sheriff flipped open a small phone and spoke into it. He smiled and nodded, apparently agreeable to everything being said to him, obviously nothing that had to do with Lori.

He closed the phone and looked around. "Jim, take over here, finish things up. I gotta go back to town, see Hizzoner." He straightened his hat and tramped out of the cordoned area, passing near Maggie but barely glancing at her. He had questioned her already. She held no interest to him anymore.

Maggie looked back at the area where Lori still lay. She knew now why she didn't want to leave. Someone had to be here for Lori. Someone who cared. Maggie wasn't family, but at least she thought of Lori as a person, not an inanimate victim of a crime whose sole remaining purpose was to provide clues leading to the perpetrator.

She shoved her hands in her pockets and looked around at the ever-changing, milling crowd of people. It was a mixed group of hotel guests mingled with employees, some talking in low voices, some silent, all with expressions of awed curiosity. Then she saw a young girl standing alone, wearing a hotel waitress uniform. She was staring in the same direction Maggie had just been, and her eyes were wet, the tip of her nose red. Maggie almost smiled. Lori wasn't so alone after all.

Someone touched her arm and she turned. It was Dyna. "How're you doing?"

"Okay."

Looking over at the crime scene area, Maggie saw that they seemed to be finished and were preparing to take Lori away. She glanced up at Dyna's face and realized she was fairly shaken up, maybe more so than Maggie.

"What do you think about going back to the hotel?" Maggie asked.

A faint look of tired relief passed over Dyna's face, and Maggie knew she must have been staying around for her sake. Maggie was surprised, and grateful. She suggested getting some dinner.

"Great!" Dyna said, some of the liveliness returning to her eyes. "But I'd say not in the dining room here. We don't need more crowds. How about room service?"

"Sounds good to me," Maggie said.

They quietly pushed through the crowd of onlookers and officials. As they walked back down the path to the hotel, Maggie became aware of an almost overwhelming fatigue. Relaxing in her quiet room with dinner was just what she needed. And she was glad she wouldn't be alone. She glanced over at Dyna's healthy-looking face and at the crystal earrings bouncing at each side of it and felt better, at least a little.

"How about some wine with the soup and sandwiches?" Dyna asked, holding the phone. They were in Maggie's room, and Dyna thumbed through the menu as she waited to be put through to room service.

"Sounds good to me," Maggie said. She pulled off her shoes and stretched out on the dark blue bedspread, feeling an exhaustion she had never known before. She knew it was more mental than physical. She propped up the pillows against the headboard and leaned her head against them, closing her eyes.

Dyna put the order through and hung up the phone. She sat on one of the two chairs at the round table near the window, dragging the other chair with her foot to use as a hassock.

"So, I heard you telling the sheriff you're a school-teacher." She stretched out her tanned legs comfortably. "What do you teach?"

"Math. Geometry, algebra, and trig."

"Yuk!" Dyna made a face.

"No, not yuk. I enjoy it." Maggie looked at Dyna, aware from the expression on her face that her statement might just as well have been, "Root canals? I love them."

"What about you?" she asked Dyna. "What do you do when you're not playing tennis?"

Dyna crossed her feet at the ankles and stretched out her arms. "At the moment," she grinned, "I guess you could say I'm at liberty. I just left my last job, in a pet store, at the manager's suggestion. He wasn't crazy about the way I lectured one of his customers for wearing a fur coat. Imagine, though, coming into a pet store with dead animal skins on your back! Also, I tended to send potential customers to the SPCA for puppies or kittens instead of selling his purebreds.

"Before that I worked in a paranormal bookshop, which was kind of fun. My folks weren't too crazy about it, but they thought at least it was an improvement from when I studied witchcraft—*good* witchcraft you understand. The only really true witchcraft." Dyna's expression was reverent for a moment, then turned rueful. "But I decided I didn't have it in me to be a successful witch."

"Problem is, I guess, I don't really *have* to do anything. Grandma Hall left me a trust fund, you see, and I only take jobs to try to please my parents. They're very busy, productive people. Dad's an engineer, and Mom designs jewelry. Maybe someday I'll find something that seems worth the effort." Dyna grinned, but didn't look convinced that that day would ever come.

Maggie wondered what life would be like without a central, motivating passion. She had always delighted in the challenge of math, and though teaching it was occasionally frustrating, she loved that too. She felt sorry for her well-to-do friend.

Dyna's grin faded and she said, "So you knew that girl out there?"

Maggie let out a long sigh. "Yes. She was in one of my geometry classes. A good kid." She shifted the pillows and sat up on the bed, leaning against them.

"Was she?"

"Yeah. Quiet, but not in a shy way. She just wasn't a bouncy cheerleader type. She was more thoughtful, introspective. And idealistic."

"Yeah?"

Maggie nodded. "I tutored her for a while, after school. She was bright in other subjects, but had some trouble with math. She wanted good grades to get into college. I remember she talked about wanting to join the Peace Corps someday. The only problem she had with it was that she hated the thought of leaving her folks. I think they weren't too well-off, and she felt maybe she should get a good job and help them out. They moved from Baltimore to this area just before her junior year.

"I met them a few times before that, when one or the other of them would pick her up after the tutoring session. Nice, decent people. I think life was a stuggle for them, but they did their best, and they were proud of her." Maggie looked out the window at a distant mountain peak. "Who knows what she would have done with her life, if she'd been given the chance?"

"Yeah," Dyna said, following Maggie's gaze, then turning back. "She sounds like a good kid. God, seventeen, eighteen, is that what she was? How can someone die, like that, so young? How do their parents handle something so awful?"

Maggie thought of her own parents. They had wanted her to be with them this week at the beach. Had she been selfish to say no, to do her own thing? Look how it had turned out. They would be horrified to find out what she had run into, but what had happened to her was nothing compared to Lori. What if they had to receive the kind of news Lori's folks would be getting?

Guilt tweaked at her when she thought of the worry that would come when they found out. She would have to call and tell them. They would want her to leave, pack up, join everyone at Bethany. And she could do that.

But then she thought of Lori's parents. Their lives had been shattered. Their daughter had been murdered. And by whom? Nobody seemed to know yet. And Maggie wondered just how much would be done to find out. The sheriff had seemed more concerned with other things. Maybe she could do more by staying?

She looked back at Dyna. Dyna's expression was angry, which seemed strangely out of place on her, as though the muscles had to rearrange in ways they had never tried before.

"Whoever killed her really deserves the worst," Dyna said. "The chair, hanging—whatever we have here in Maryland. I just hope that sheriff catches the creep soon. They will, don't you think?"

Maggie wished she could agree, and let it go at that. But she never was one who could just go along with the easy answer. It had caused her problems in the past, and she had a feeling it was going to cause her more in the future. She shook her head in disagreement.

"I'm not so sure about that."

Chapter Six

"How soon did they say they'd send up our dinner?" Maggie asked, moving off the bed, stretching restlessly.

As if in answer to her question she heard the doors to the elevator down the hall open, and footsteps clicked toward their room, accompanied by the muffled clatter of dishes and cutlery. Dyna was up and across the room at the sound of the first knock and a voice calling, "Room service!"

She opened the door to a heavy set woman with salt-and-pepper hair which mirrored her black and white uniform. The woman picked up a large silver-domed tray from a cart and stepped into the room, walking slowly and carefully, but when Maggie moved forward with an offer of help, the woman shook her head with a laugh.

"Oh! No need. It's not all that heavy. I'm just being careful so as not to spill the soup." She set the tray onto the table and, with a practiced smoothness, pulled off the silver dome, releasing enticing aromas.

"There! Haven't carried one of those in a while. I've been supervisor the last few years. But they're in such a mess down in the kitchen, what with that awful thing happening to one of their girls. . . ." She paused, taking a breath. "I decided to bring this up myself, otherwise you young ladies would be waiting a good long time, and you don't need that after all you've already gone through." She smiled, looking at them with a maternal eye.

"Thank you," Maggie said, signing the bill and handing it to her, along with the tip. "That was very kind of you." Maggie *was* grateful, but not altogether pleased to find out she and Dyna had acquired a kind of celebrity.

"Not at all." The woman nodded her own thanks and pushed the tip into a pocket pulled tight over wide hips. "And if you need anything while you're with us, you can ask for me: Burnelle. I'll try to take special care of you while you're here. That is, if you *are* staying on, I mean, after what's happened?"

Maggie knew how she felt, but didn't know about Dyna. She looked over at her, eyebrows raised questioningly.

Dyna shrugged. "If you're staying, I will too. I've got nothing to hurry back to, and I've got a feeling hotel security will be super-tight now. We'll probably be safer here than back in the streets of Baltimore."

Maggie wasn't so sure about that, but she thought she would stay for at least a couple days, maybe more. She didn't know if it was just stubbornness to stick with her original plan of vacationing on her own, or something else. She turned back to Burnelle.

"I guess we won't go rushing off just yet."

"Well, I'm glad. We hate to see you going away with only bad memories of our Highview. But it surely was a terrible thing. That poor, sweet girl. I wondered, what did the sheriff have to say about who done it?"

Dyna was already digging hungrily into her dinner and answered between chews and swallows.

"Not much. But . . . I gathered they didn't have a lot to go on. *I* think it was probably some psycho lurking in the woods there."

"Oh! My!" Burnelle shook her head. "And to think it could have been *any* one, or more than one of our girls. They seem to be always wandering around back there, smoking their cigarettes. And of course, flirtin' with that tennis fellow, the good-looking one. Though some said there was something going on between him and that poor girl who was killed, and I wondered. . . . Well, never mind that. That's just idle gossip, and I don't believe in gossip. Did they find footprints, or some kind of evidence?" She pronounced it ev-*ee*-dence.

"No," Maggie said. "I don't think they really have much so far. Umm, is there a corkscrew or something for this?" She held up the wine bottle, whose cork was deeply imbedded.

Burnelle took the bottle from her and pulled a corkscrew from her apron pocket. She deftly worked in the screw and pulled out the cork. Then she reached over for the two stemmed glasses on the tray and poured out wine for each of them.

"I don't usually approve of young ladies and alcohol," she said, her lips pursed primly as she poured, "but I appreciate the strain you have been under. We'll consider this something of a tonic, to help you sleep better tonight." Burnelle nodded with a tolerant smile as she said this, and Maggie reached for her glass with mixed feelings.

She knew she had agreed to the wine when Dyna suggested it exactly for the "tonic" reason. Her nerves were jangled, and a few sips of wine would help. She certainly didn't want it for celebrating. But now she felt she had just received a disapproving, motherly raised eyebrow and felt annoyance rising. This was the kind of thing she had come here to get away from.

She caught Dyna looking at her, laughter dancing in her

eyes above the chicken sandwich she held to her mouth, and her irritation changed to an overwhelming urge to laugh. She looked away from Dyna and sucked at her cheeks for control.

"Well, thank you, uh, Burnelle. And we'll, ah, certainly remember to call you if we need anything."

Burnelle smiled and nodded, and, wiping her hands on the sides of her uniform dress, moved toward the door.

"Yes, you do that. Be sure you do. Now, I'd better get back downstairs and see what needs doing. Lord knows, most of the people around here have just gone to pieces. Someone has to see that the things that need doing get done. Enjoy your dinner."

Maggie called, "Thanks," as Burnelle edged out the door, and Dyna raised her wine glass as a farewell salute, laughter shaking her by now. Maggie shushed her, and tried to pull her arm down, but broke down herself once Burnelle was out of sight and earshot.

Maggie was just finishing her soup, when she was startled by a brisk knock on the door.

"Yes?" she called.

"Miss Olenski? It's Kathryn Crawford, the hotel manager. May I come in?"

Maggie jumped up and opened the door to see another large woman, this one wearing a beige linen suit and chunky heels, her dark brown hair pulled up into a businesslike bun. She strode into the room with an air of authority, and smiled a tight, cool smile, her arms moving stiffly at her side. She stopped and clasped her hands together, facing Maggie.

"I just want to say how sorry we all are at Highview that you had to be involved in this extremely sad incident." She looked over to Dyna, including her.

"Thank you," Maggie answered. The woman had been courteous, but her cool manner inspired a cool response.

"It was more than an incident, though," she said. "It was a murder."

Ms. Crawford's eyelids flickered. "Yes, of course. Very unfortunate. And unnecessary. I don't know how many times I've warned our young girls not to go off alone into the woods. But some of them are foolishly headstrong, I'm afraid."

Maggie wouldn't have described Lori as either foolish or headstrong, but she said nothing.

"I see you've had your dinner. I was going to suggest you dine downstairs, on us, after what you've gone through, but since you've had room service, I'll just see that there's no charge."

"Thank you. That's very nice."

Ms. Crawford nodded and walked to the door. "I hope you'll continue your stay with us?"

"Yes, I think we both plan to stay."

The woman smiled. "Good. We'll do our best to make the rest of your holiday pleasant. Good day." She nodded and swept out the door. Maggie looked over at Dyna.

"Well, I guess we just had a complimentary dinner," she said.

"Mmm. Seems to me, she could have easily made it a free vacation, what with all you just went through, and her not wanting you to bad-mouth the place back home and all."

Maggie nodded. "She probably is pretty stressed out herself right now." She shrugged and looked back at the closed door. "But then again, maybe she didn't really *want* us to stay."

Dyna soon left to shower in her own room, and Maggie decided to take a warm, oil-scented bath. It was a luxury she seldom had time for, but when she did make the time she often found that as well as unwinding tense muscles, a hot bath helped to untangle jumbled thoughts. She filled the tub and slipped in with a sigh, leaning her head back against a thick towel propped on the edge.

Another thing that helped her relax, besides passing the time on long car rides, was number games. Maggie stared at the beige, square tiles that covered the walls above her as she lay back in the tub. She lazily counted the rows up and the rows across, multiplied, and got the total number. As the steam floated above her head she estimated the size of the squares and calculated the area of wall that was covered. Still soaking comfortably, she next began to figure the amount of adhesive that would be needed to cover that area, if it were spread at a thickness of one-eighth inch. When the tiles began to steam up and her eyes to droop, she knew she had had enough.

Well soaked, mildly puckered, and definitely relaxed, Maggie toweled off, wrapped herself in a robe, and looked at the time. She knew she had to call her folks at Bethany sometime, answer her mother's message, and she supposed this was as good a time as any. With a sigh she sat down at the phone, stared at it for a few moments, then picked up the receiver and punched in the numbers. She listened to the rings with a tightness in her body which relaxed when she heard the voice of her younger brother.

"Joe! It's me, Maggie."

"Hey, Maggie. How's it going?"

Maggie heard the usual laid-back tone to her brother's voice, and hated to spoil his mood with her news. As an older sister she had always felt somewhat protective of him, even though he had fought that attitude tooth and nail all their lives, preferring, she felt, to think *he* was the protector. She had often wondered if that was the reason they always got along as well as they did, because the only thing they fought over was who was looking after whom.

"Are Mom and Dad there?" she asked.

"No, they went out to dinner with Aunt Sophie. Too bad you missed them."

Maggie heard the light teasing in his voice and laughed. He knew her well.

"Mom called here," she said, "wanting to know if I arrived okay, so I guess you can tell her I did." She paused, deciding what to say. "I might be leaving sooner than I thought, though. I don't know yet."

"Why, what's wrong?" Joe's voice was suddenly serious, picking up on her tone.

She told him, then, what had happened, trying to be as detached as possible, but not succeeding totally. Her voice shook when she said that the victim was Lori, her former student.

"Maggie, get out of there," Joe said. "Even if you lose whatever you paid so far, get out of there. Come here, or go back to Baltimore. Just get out. Tonight."

Joe's ordering manner suddenly annoyed her. She would make her own decisions. She hadn't called for advice. "Joe," she said, "I want to see Lori's parents. They must live around here."

"Maggie . . ." Joe protested, his tone exasperated.

"It's the least I can do. I feel I have to do *something*. I'll probably leave soon, so don't worry."

"Don't worry!"

"Right, and Joe, maybe you shouldn't tell the folks right away. It'll only spoil their vacation. I'll tell them when I see them. After I've left here. Okay?"

"Maggie, what if they read about it in the paper?"

"They're on vacation, Joe. Have you ever seen either of them pick up the paper at the beach? Besides, I doubt that this will get much publicity beyond this area."

"Maggie. . . ."

"I'll let you know what I'm doing, I promise. I'll probably see you soon." Maggie wasn't sure if Joe picked up on the "probably," but she hung up quickly before he could badger her on it. She didn't know what she planned to do herself, and didn't want to be pinned down to any promises. She felt a twinge of guilt at putting Joe off, but told herself she would check in with him again soon. He would just have to be patient.

She sat by the phone and looked around the room, wondering what to do next. It was too soon to just go to bed, and she didn't feel like sitting alone in her room. She was too keyed-up now, and knew she'd never be able to concentrate on television or any of the paperbacks she had brought with her. She decided to dress and go down to the main, social floor of the Inn.

A quick call to Dyna's room a few minutes later got no answer, so she tucked her key card into the pocket of her slacks and left the room, not knowing what she was looking for except perhaps a little more distraction than her television could provide.

Her first step off the elevator lowered her hopes. The lobby was deserted except for two whispering employees behind the desk. The women looked up as Maggie came near and waited to see if she wanted something. She merely smiled a greeting, which was returned, and walked on, hearing the whispering resume behind her.

A glance out the tall windows showed the lawns beyond, floodlit, with a uniformed guard in sight. Maggie felt no temptation to leave the relative security that walls and locked doors offered tonight, and continued down the hall. The dining room was nearly empty, only one or two tables still occupied by lingering couples sipping coffee. The soft sound of music drew Maggie's attention farther down, and she came to a small cocktail lounge. She stepped in.

The music came from a jukebox, a slow melancholy country song. A small bandstand was vacant, and four or five people sat at scattered tables, talking quietly or just staring at the jukebox or their drink. No one seemed to notice or care particularly when Maggie walked in, and as she didn't see Dyna, the one person she knew here so far, she went to the small bar and sat down alone.

A bartender came over and smiled. "Hi there. What'll you have?"

"Club soda, with lime," she ordered.

He poured it out for her, and slid over a bowl of nuts. As Maggie took small sips and nibbled, she looked at all the pictures on the wall in back of the bar, read and reread all the advertisements, and gradually began to wonder if this was really better than sitting upstairs watching television. The country song was replaced by another one, slower and sadder.

Another young woman walked in and sat a few stools away from her, leaning her arms onto the bar. She wore the hotel waitress uniform covered partially with a light jacket, and she reached for a pack of cigarettes in one pocket and tapped out one slightly bent cigarette.

"Hey, Dave, got any free beers for me tonight?"

"In your dreams, Babe," he said, grinning. "You still working?"

"Nah. It's so slow, Roz told me to take off."

"Yeah, it's the same here. I think we'll be closing up early." Neither of them said the reason out loud, but Maggie could feel it hanging in the air: a girl had been murdered; Lori Basker had been murdered. She picked up a peanut from the dish, and looked away from them.

The bartender, Dave, wandered to the other end of the bar and stooped down, checking the stock. Maggie felt the waitress's eyes on her and turned her head back. The young woman smiled, and pointed to the dish of nuts. "Mind if I have a few? They're all I can afford tonight."

Maggie smiled back and said, "Sure," sliding the bowl between them. The waitress moved over one stool and grabbed a handful of nuts, pushing half into her mouth. She was small and slim, with dark, frizzy-curly hair framing her face. Her bright red lipstick left prints on the end of her cigarette. A nametag pinned near her collar said "Holly." Maggie recognized her now as the girl with the teary face she had seen at the tennis courts, watching them bundle up Lori's body.

Holly looked at Maggie closely and said, "You're the one found Lori, aren't you?"

Maggie nodded.

"I saw them talking to you," Holly continued. "Must've been pretty bad, huh?"

"Uh-huh," Maggie agreed. "I guess you worked with her?"

"Yeah. Nice kid."

Maggie guessed that Lori might have been all of two or three years younger than Holly. It evidently was enough for Holly to consider her "the kid."

"She just started here," Holly said, "last month, for the summer. She was going to college, and was always reading books and things during her breaks."

"Was she?"

"Yeah, must have been smart. She didn't hang around with the rest of us, but then we didn't know her too long."

Maggie remembered the tears she had seen on Holly's face and thought Lori had evidently made at least a small dent into Holly's life.

"Was she seeing anyone? I mean, someone mentioned she might have been seeing the tennis pro, Rob, uh, Clayton. Was that right?"

"Why, you got your eye on him?" Holly laughed, then suddenly seemed to remember they were talking about a murder and stopped. "Wouldn't blame you, half the girls around here do. But I don't know if Lori was seeing him. Can't say I ever saw them together. She did disappear every so often, now that I think of it, but I don't know if she was meeting someone. Why, was the sheriff asking questions?"

"No, the sheriff didn't ask many questions at all, except for the obvious ones. He seems to be a busy man, maybe too busy for solving murders." As soon as she said it, Maggie realized how foolish it must sound. After all, that was the sheriff's job. How could he be too busy to do his job properly? Busy with what? She noticed, however, that Holly wasn't looking at her as if she had lost her mind.

"Hah!" Holly hooted. "That sounds like Sheriff Burger all right. The only thing he has a lot of time for is getting himself re-elected. My guess is he's going to try to pin it on some bum he finds passed out somewhere. That, and keep it all as quiet as he can. Bad publicity for the hotel, you know. He gets a hefty donation for his campaigns from the owners."

"Oh?" Maggie's eyebrows went up, but she was unsure how seriously to take this information. Could a sheriff really be that lax?

"Uh-huh." Holly nodded firmly. "You know, this isn't the first time something's happened around here." She paused and glanced around, continuing in a lowered voice and leaning toward Maggie.

"One of the girls, Melanie—this was when I first started here, about two years ago—was found dead in her room here one morning from an overdose of sleeping pills. The sheriff called it a suicide, but most people that knew her didn't believe that. They said there was no reason for her to kill herself. She wasn't depressed—for cripe's sake, she was thinking of getting married! And nobody remembered her ever taking sleeping pills either. It's like they suddenly appeared out of nowhere."

Maggie shook her head, frowning. "That isn't really like what happened to Lori today. She was clearly murdered."

"Yeah, I know. Sheriff can't call it suicide 'cause no one's going to bash their own head in—sorry," she said, as Maggie winced. "I know there's no proof that Melanie *didn't* kill herself, but believe me, there's still a real creepy feeling hanging around here about it. Like, maybe someone got away with murder."

Maggie looked at the young waitress speculatively. She had an intense, wary expression on her thin face, like a young deer, Maggie thought, alert to danger. "Why do you stay here if you're so concerned?"

"The money. Can't find a job that pays as good around here. And I really need it right now. But as soon as I get enough of a stake saved up, believe me, I'll be out of here."

Dave, the bartender had moved closer and cleared his throat, trying to get Holly's attention, but she didn't seem to notice.

"And if I were you," she went on to Maggie, "I'd go to some other place to vacation. Someplace. . . ." She noticed Maggie looking past her shoulder and turned to see Kathryn Crawford standing a few feet away in the open doorway. The older woman stood stiffly, frowning her displeasure.

"Holly, aren't you on duty now?"

"No ma'm. Roz told me to take off early."

"I see." The manager's gaze left Holly and moved to Maggie. She managed a smile, but it didn't reach her eyes. "Good evening, Miss Olenski."

Maggie nodded, feeling the tension in the air between Holly and Ms. Crawford, wishing she could do or say something to relieve it but unable to think of anything.

Ms. Crawford turned and walked down the hall. Holly made a face at her back. "She probably heard me tell you to get out of here. She's been here so long she thinks of the place as hers and can't stand hearing anyone bad-mouth it. She needs to get a life. Her and her daughter eat, sleep, and breathe Highview."

"She has a daughter working here too?"

"Yeah, she's her assistant. Talk about nek . . . nes. . . . ?"

"Nepotism?"

"Yeah. Anyway, you know she got her job because of her mother, and she's not any older than any of us waitresses. But Miss High-and-Mighty Crawford can't lower herself to speak to us, except to point out what we did wrong, of course." Holly jabbed her cigarette out in the ashtray with some vehemence.

"Um, Holly, do you happen to know where Lori's family lives?"

Holly shook her head. "No, but I could find out for you easy. Why—you want to go see them?"

Maggie nodded. "I taught Lori when she was in tenth grade and got to know her folks a little. They sent me a couple Christmas cards after they moved to this area, but I don't remember the address. They were good people. I'd like to talk to them. Maybe there's something I can do."

Holly nodded, her face solemn. She stood up to leave, and reached for a final handful of nuts. "I can probably get it to you by tomorrow. And, uh, look, maybe don't worry too much about everything I said, okay? I mean, I'm just kind of upset and all. My boyfriend says I get too hyper about things." She flashed a quick grin. "So anyway, maybe, just forget it, okay?"

"Okay." Maggie smiled back at her. She watched the young waitress leave, turning in the opposite direction Kathryn Crawford had gone, and thought about their conversation. Was Holly's version of an earlier death colored by today's tragedy, she wondered, or had there really been another murder at the Highview? And was her opinion of Sheriff Burger justified?

She didn't know the girl well enough to answer those questions for herself yet, but she knew they would be two more contributions to a restless night. She sighed and finished the last of her soda, felt for the key card tucked in her pocket, and headed for the elevator. She wondered, as she walked, if her skin could take another soaking bubble bath or not.

Chapter Seven

May 23, 1997

Melanie was bushed. Working the evening shift was good for tips, but hard work. She didn't realize how tough waitressing could be. She thought she was in good shape, but now she seemed to be tired all the time. Would these high-energy pills help?

Guaranteed—that's what she'd been told. All natural, too. Everyone here at the Highview took them—that's what she was told too. Well, she sure needed something. And they didn't cost her anything, either. She'd just take a couple. . . .

Melanie didn't hear the door to her room open as she rinsed shampoo out of her hair in the shower. So she didn't hear the pills being dropped into the diet soda by her bed, the soda she always sipped as she watched David Letterman, unwinding before she turned out the lights and went to sleep.

Tonight she would watch David Letterman, and she would turn out her light sooner than usual, yawns overtaking her. She would sleep the soundest she had ever slept, never knowing that it would be the final sleep of her life. She wouldn't hear the screams of the girl who eventually came to wake her, long past her usual rising time. The girl who *couldn't* wake her, because Melanie was dead.

Chapter Eight

June 19, 1999

Maggie drove down a portion of the same winding road she had driven up the previous day on her way to the Inn. As the posts of the guardrail rushed by, she reflected on how quickly, and how drastically, her expectations for this week's vacation had changed.

Twenty-four hours ago she thought she faced seven days of relaxation and recreation. She hoped to leave all major problems behind her in Baltimore. Suddenly, overnight, those problems had shrunk considerably in importance next to the horrifying one that had loomed up. One of her former students had been murdered. She, Maggie, had found the body. And now she would be facing the parents of that girl. Exams, grades, fussy principals, and demanding parents paled by comparison.

Holly had slipped Maggie the Basker family's address as she and Dyna ate breakfast in the hotel's dining room, adding a few brief directions in a low voice as she poured coffee into Maggie's cup.

"I got this from Crawford's files, which she usually guards like a dragon, so keep it to yourself, okay?"

Maggie promised she would and thanked her.

"Want me to go along?" Dyna asked. She sat across the table from Maggie, wearing hot pink spandex bicycle shorts with an oversized T-shirt. Beaded earrings brushed her shoulders.

Maggie declined, but not because of Dyna's costume of the day, although it *was* somewhat inappropriate for a condolence call. She worried that even her own visit might be too intrusive, that Lori's mother wouldn't remember who she was. But she still wanted to see her if she could, even if only briefly.

As she drove, Maggie wondered what she would say. She had gone to funerals and wakes before, of course, but she realized it had almost always been in the company of her family. Aged relatives, older friends of her parents had died, invariably of natural causes, and Maggie's role had been simply to be there, a sympathetic presence, while the older generation did most of the talking.

There seemed to be a set script for those events: platitudes and expressions of sympathy that rolled out easily. Those deaths had been expected, usually peaceful, and sometimes a relief for all concerned, including the deceased. There was never the horror that was connected with Lori's death. What platitudes could she offer on the murder of a daughter?

Maggie felt the stomach tremor return, an echo of the one she had had at the crime scene. She suddenly wished intensely that her mother were here with her now, and Maggie could simply shift the burden to her.

Her wish surprised her. For the past several days Maggie had done her best to put distance between her mother and all the other family members who had gone down together to Bethany. It wasn't simply the vacation plans that she had rebelled against. It was their whole attitude toward her. In her parents eyes, she was still their little girl. She had been earning her own money teaching for three years now and had her own apartment—which was another major crisis in the Olenski household—but they still refused to accept her as an adult. Maggie didn't know what it would take, but she was doing her darnedest to find out.

Part of the problem, she understood, was her parents' background. They had both grown up in the same neighborhood in Baltimore, surrounded by grandparents, aunts and uncles, and cousins. They had each lived at home until they married, turning over their paychecks to their own parents and receiving allowances in return. Maybe they couldn't think of Maggie as grown up until she got married. If that were the case, then she would have a long-running battle ahead, as there was no prospective bridegroom in the picture, and Maggie felt in no hurry to find one.

She reached into the bag of sourballs in her console and rooted around with a quick sideways glance until she found her favorite—Tangy Grape. She unwrapped it and popped it in her mouth, and felt her stomach tremors ease just a bit.

She saw the sign for Coopersburg, where the Baskers lived, and followed it onto a road to the right. The little town was not all that far from the Highview. From what Maggie could tell as she drove into it, with its collection of small businesses and drably modest storefronts, the Inn was likely a major source of income for many of its citizens, either as employment or as a consumer of some of their supplies or services.

The Inn possibly drew from several such small towns surrounding the area. If that were the case, Maggie could *almost* understand the sheriff's desire to keep the Inn's reputation intact by downplaying any unpleasant incidents that occurred there, if in fact he had. Campaign contributions from the owners might be a major concern, but preserving an economy and way of life might be just as important. Whichever it was, though, selfish or unselfish motivation, the end result—suppression of the truth—was just as unacceptable.

Maggie checked the address on the slip of paper Holly had given her and recalled what she had said.

" 'Green Street should cross Main where the laundromat is, and there's a tavern across the street in a yellow building. I don't know if you go right or left on Green, but it shouldn't be too hard to find.' "

Maggie found the street, decided on a left turn, and located the house within two blocks. As she pulled next to the curb, she noticed several other cars parked nearby, and realized she would not be the only one making a condolence call at this time. She had another anxious thought that perhaps she would be intruding, and considered just pulling away, turning around, and going right back to the Highview.

Her mother's voice in her head stopped her. "People don't want to be left alone at times like this." Anna Olenski had said it many times, and Maggie remembered helping her wrap freshly baked bread or fix a casserole to take to a friend or relative in mourning. "They need a little kindness to take away the hurt."

Maggie didn't have a loaf of bread or a casserole, so she would have to do her best on her own. "All right, Mom, you win this time," she said aloud. "But I'll take it from here, okay?"

Maggie climbed out of her car and walked up the steps to the porch of the frame house. The porch could have used a little paint, but it was otherwise in good shape. The house was an old frame clapboard, two stories and a high attic. A chain link fence surrounded the backyard, and a medium-

sized, multi-breed tan dog was beyond it; he barked duti-
fully at her once or twice.

Maggie's knock was answered by a grim, large-sized,
middle-aged woman. She wore a flower-printed blouse
stretched over the top of navy polyester pants, and her dark
hair framed a face that bore no resemblance to Mrs. Basker's, as Maggie remembered it. She looked at Maggie
stonily, blocking the door with her bulk, and asked, "Yes?"
in an unwelcoming tone.

"Ah, I'm Maggie Olenski. I was Lori's math teacher in
high school. If this is a bad time, I certainly understand. . . ."

"Oh! Come in, dear, come in." The stern face meta-
morphosed into that of a generic, kindly aunt, and she
pulled Maggie by the arm through the doorway, moving
back several steps to make room. "I was afraid you were
one of those reporters. It's been terrible. How they can
bother people with questions at a time like this. 'How do
you feel?' How do they think we feel! So," she said to
Maggie in a softened tone with a hint of reverence, "you
teach up there at the high school?"

"No, actually I teach in Baltimore. I had Lori in class
when she lived there."

Maggie had stepped into the living room, and she saw
Lori's mother sitting on the sofa. She was being attended
to by another large woman who dwarfed Mrs. Basker's own
small frame. The larger woman was alternately rubbing the
grieving woman's hand and moving offerings of food, coffee, and Kleenex a fraction of an inch closer on the coffee
table in front of her. The aroma of perking coffee drifted
in from the kitchen. Lori's mother looked up and stared
blankly at Maggie.

"Mrs. Basker, I'm Maggie Olenski. I taught—"

Mrs. Basker's blank face relaxed to a soft, sad-eyed
smile. She stood up with a slight unsteadiness and reached
out to Maggie. "Miss Olenski. Yes, I remember. How kind.
Lori always . . . Marlene, would you get a cup for Miss

Olenski?" she said to the woman at her left in a small voice. "Come, sit down." She motioned to Maggie. "So kind."

Maggie took the vacated spot on the sofa, and Lori's mother sat beside her. The older woman pushed at wisps of gray-brown hair around her face and immediately offered some of the small sandwiches and cookies on the table with anxious, jerky movements. Maggie hesitated, then saw that accepting something would please the woman, so she took a vanilla wafer.

"Lori was a very special student of mine," Maggie began, "a very special girl. I'm so sorry . . ." She broke off, her voice unsteady, and Mrs. Basker gripped her hand in both of her own.

"I know, I know, dear."

Maggie looked into this grieving mother's eyes, and saw the pain deep inside them, thinly veiled by a lifetime of conventions and habits, habits that placed immediate concern for her visitor over her own distress. She felt that was harder to take than a flood of tears would have been.

Marlene emerged from the kitchen carrying a cup of coffee for Maggie, and set it on the table in front of her. Maggie gave a quick smile of thanks, and Lori's mother moved the sugar closer, half rising when she thought Maggie might want cream which wasn't there, only relaxing when Maggie assured her she didn't need it.

A tall man whose freckled face resembled Lori's more than her mother's stood near the doorway of the kitchen, and Maggie recognized him as Mr. Basker. He was quietly listening to the murmurs of a shorter man clad in overalls whom he gazed at with solemn, sunken eyes.

Mrs. Basker cleared her throat gently and said, "Did you drive all the way up here from Baltimore, dear?"

"Not today. I arrived yesterday, to stay at the Highview."

"Oh, I see." Mrs. Basker seemed to be struggling to place that piece of information into its proper niche.

Maggie took a deep breath. "Mrs. Basker, I'm the one who found Lori."

"Oh!" Her hand flew to her mouth as the thought of all that implied became clear. Maggie saw her grapple with it, feeling some of her anguish, and wishing she hadn't had to be the cause of it. The fact would have come out sometime though, she knew, in news reports, or hearsay, and perhaps it was just as well to get it over with. Who could say? All she knew was this woman, this family, had a long road of healing ahead, and maybe it was best to clear it now of as much debris as possible.

After what seemed like a long silence, Mrs. Basker's hand reached out for Maggie's again. "I'm sorry for you, but I'm glad for Lori's sake that you were there for her. I'd like to think she knew, somehow. She always liked you so much." She looked at Maggie with pain-filled eyes, the veil now dropped, and whispered, "Who killed her? Who killed my little girl?" Two large tears moved slowly down her face, and Maggie could only shake her head helplessly.

She didn't know.

As more people arrived at the Baskers', Maggie rose to leave. Some quick introductions, a few more words, then she made her way to the door, escorted by the same large woman who had admitted her, Lori's Aunt Rose. Aunt Rose came out onto the front porch with her, pulling the door closed behind her, thanking her for coming.

"You staying on at the Highview?" Rose asked as Maggie started to step down.

"Yes, at least for now."

"It's a nice place," Rose said politely, her face not quite agreeing with her words. "Did the town a lot of good when it got built up there." Rose heaved a sigh and settled down onto an old metal porch chair. She pulled a handkerchief out of her sleeve and wiped at her face.

Maggie sat down on the top step. "I was talking to someone last night who works there. She said Lori's wasn't the first death at the Highview, that another girl died of an overdose of pills which the sheriff called a suicide."

"Yes, yes, I remember," Rose said, shaking her head. "A terrible thing. I didn't know the girl. But it's always a terrible thing when someone so . . ." Rose's gaze moved to the oak tree standing tall and silent at the edge of the yard. She was quiet for a few moments, then sighed. "Death shouldn't come violently, especially not to the young. It should come quietly, like a friend, when one has finished all one has to do and is tired and ready to go. Don't you think?"

Rose turned her round eyes to Maggie and smiled sadly, and Maggie could only nod. She had never thought much about death before, and now it seemed to be all-pervasive.

"You didn't know anything in particular about the other girl's death, then?" Maggie asked, bringing the conversation back from the philosophical to the pragmatic.

"No, but I knew about poor Randy Chamber's accident."

"Randy Chamber? Who was he?"

Rose waved a large arm pointing vaguely to the right. "Our neighbor's boy. Worked up there too. In maintenance. He was driving home late one night, on that awful twisty road, went off it, and was killed. Police said he was driving recklessly, but . . ." Rose shook her head with disbelief. "He was a good boy, not one of those wild ones."

Maggie stared. A *second* suspicious death. Or was it?

"Did the sheriff investigate it?" she asked.

Rose nodded. "But you know how it is. Just another teenager wrecking his car, getting himself killed. They said there was nothing else to it. Who can tell? All I know is it was awful hard on his folks."

Rose pushed herself heavily out of the chair. "Well, I'd better get back in, see what needs doing."

"Oh, by the way," Maggie said, stopping Rose in midturn, "what was Lori studying in college? Was it biology?"

"Biology? No, Lori wanted to be a social worker. She wanted to help people. She wanted to get a degree, starting first at the community college, then finishing the last two years at the university."

"Was she taking any summer classes, do you know, perhaps a science class?"

"No, she had to work full-time in the summer to pay for tuition. The Highview was the best job, the best pay." Rose's face had a question mark on it.

"There was a book found near her," Maggie explained. "A college level biology book. Not exactly light summer reading, so I wondered if she needed it for a class." Maggie supposed it meant nothing. More important, probably, were the people Lori saw. "What about friends?" she asked. "Did she go out much, have a boyfriend?"

"Oh, she had friends," Rose said, "but she wasn't what you'd call the party type. I think she had a boyfriend back in high school, but that broke up some time ago. I never heard anything about a boyfriend lately, but that doesn't mean there wasn't one.

"She was a good girl," the older woman went on. "Cared about her friends, and about people in general, something you don't see a lot in the young ones. Just last month she helped out at the local blood drive. They had it at the community center and quite a few people from the hotel came to donate, which I'll bet she had a lot to do with. And she used to babysit for free, off and on, for the Parkinsons over on Gibson Road, who were having a hard time of things. No, you don't see a lot of that."

Rose heaved a mighty sigh. "Well, they say the good die young. Must be why I'm still around." She gave a sharp laugh. "I guess I'd better go back in."

She looked at Maggie silently for a few moments. "You take care, now, up there." Rose's face was solemn. She opened the door and disappeared into the house, and Maggie stood on the porch for a while, then turned and walked slowly down the steps.

Back in her car, Maggie sat for a moment, her mind sorting through the odd bits of information it had been accumulating. Things at the Highview, beyond Lori's death, seemed out of kilter. Holly had told her about the presumed suicide, and now Rose mentioned an accidental death. Was there any connection between these deaths and Lori's? She couldn't know yet, but it was disturbing. The only thing she knew right now was that Lori's mother deserved an answer to her plea: "Who killed my little girl?" Lori's entire family deserved an honest answer.

Maggie checked the map, then started the car and turned it around toward Main Street. Main would take her to Highway 42. This in turn would lead her to the sheriff's office. If anyone would have an answer to that question, the sheriff should. And if not, Maggie wanted to know just what he was doing to get it.

Chapter Nine

April 9, 1998

Randy climbed into his old, beat-up Ford. It didn't seem old and beat-up to him. To him it was great and wonderful, his ticket to independence, the envy of most of his friends. So it had a few dents and scratches—he would fix that, as well as the jerking in the transmission, and some other things, as soon as he got the money.

And he *was* getting it. Thanks to this car, he had got the job up here at the Highview, able to drive up to work part-time on landscaping. For digging a few holes and dropping in a few bushes he was getting paid more than he ever got in his life, though at seventeen he hadn't had too many jobs yet.

Randy started up the car and pulled out onto the gravel road that led to the main one down the mountain. His mind went over the day he'd had. A long day. After digging and raking for several hours, he'd been directed to work on some of the tools that had been stored all winter, scrape off rust, check the motors of the small engines and stuff. Not that he minded. It meant extra pay, and he liked doing things like that, especially the engine stuff. But it kept him late, and he and Jody might not be able to make that movie after all. Maybe if he stepped on it. . . .

Randy sped around the curves of the road. It was empty, so he wasn't worried about traffic. His tires sqealed as he took a sharp bend, and he pressed the brake as he came to another. He heard, or maybe felt, something snap, and the brake went all the way to the floor. What the heck!

Randy had just worked on those brakes two weekends ago. They should have been in great shape. But his foot kept pumping and nothing was grabbing. Randy's heart started beating hard. Another curve came up and he just barely made it. The car was going fast. Faster than he could handle. He thought he liked to drive fast, but not like this. Another curve. Then another.

The last thing he saw was the dark shapes of the trees as he crashed through the guardrail. The last thing he felt was the terrible thud as the car hit the rocky slope, then rolled. Randy's head hit something hard, and blackness replaced consciousness, which was merciful, for he wasn't aware when the flames burst out, engulfing his car, his precious car, and everything in it, including him.

Chapter Ten

Maggie parked her car at the rear of the Highview and walked across the grounds toward the back entrance of the hotel. She shoved her hands into her skirt pockets and frowned, deep in thought. As she started to veer left to the door, the sound of a familiar voice stopped her.

"Maggie! Maggie, over here!"

Maggie looked up to see Dyna waving at her from a green and white striped lounge chair beside the pool. She brightened at the sight of her ever-cheerful friend and went over to join her.

"Dyna, you're just what I need." Maggie sank into the chair next to her.

"Kinda rough seeing the family?" Dyna asked. She seemed to be trying to look properly somber, and nearly succeeded.

"Yes, but I guess I was prepared for that. I *wasn't* prepared for what I ran into later."

Maggie told Dyna about going to the sheriff's office. She

had been greeted quite cordially, invited to sit down, offered coffee. But when she inquired about the investigation into Lori's death, she got vague answers and empty-sounding assurances.

"We're working on it. Don't you worry your little head about it," was the deepest extent of his answers.

To add to her frustration, their conversation had been constantly interrupted by phone calls and questions from a deputy on various unrelated matters. When Maggie finally gave up and rose to leave, the sheriff had covered the phone with his hand and given her a friendly wink and a promise that "everything is being taken care of." Which did nothing to convince Maggie.

The sheriff reminded her too much of Harvey, her school principal. Harvey was big on talk, loaded with charm, and made promises that more often than not evaporated as quickly as he closed his office door behind you. Maggie had soon learned that if she wanted something done at school she had to find a way to do it herself. Maybe she would have to do the same here.

"You don't think they'll find the killer?" Dyna asked.

Maggie sighed. "I doubt it."

She looked over at her friend, whose multi-shaded blond hair was escaping bit by bit from the tie holding most of it near the top of her head. "I can't stand the thought of this murder not being solved, though," she said. "It wouldn't be fair to Lori's family to just leave things hanging. They deserve an answer. And something's going on here, I'm afraid. More than just a drifter attacking a defenseless girl in the woods." She told Dyna about the two other employee deaths.

"You think someone from here is killing people?" Dyna's blue eyes opened wide, and she glanced nervously around at the sparsely populated pool area. A white-haired woman wrapped in terrycloth smiled sweetly back at her from her lounge chair several feet away.

"I think *maybe* someone from here killed Lori, and if so, Sheriff Burger doesn't seem likely to find out who."

"Well, maybe we could try to find out," Dyna said.

The edges of Maggie's lips turned up in a grim smile. "Yes, that's exactly what I was thinking. Maybe we could."

"You mean it?"

"Yes, I do. We'll be here a few more days. We can certainly poke around, ask questions. That is, if you want to."

"Sure I do!"

Maggie was conscious of a feeling of relief which surprised her. She hadn't realized just how much she was counting on her friend's help. "But Dyna," she cautioned, "it would have to be very discreet. I might be wrong about someone from here being involved. And of course, I might be right, in which case it could be dangerous if we're not careful."

"Right. But it can't hurt to just ask a few questions, and keep our eyes open, can it?" Dyna replied, her eyes already bright with anticipation. "Where do we start?" She looked ready to leap from her chair into action.

"Well, I've been thinking. One person who's been mentioned so far with a hint of suspicion is the tennis pro, Rob Clayton. Remember when Burnelle brought our dinner to the room, she said she thought there might have been something going on between him and Lori? Why don't we start with him?"

"Rob Clayton. Okay." Dyna was on the edge of her chair by now. "What should we do, follow him? Watch him?"

Maggie smiled. "No, just talk to him. But in a way that seems natural, not like we're interrogating him. How about if I take a lesson from him? My backhand *is* really awful, you know."

"Yeah, I know. Good idea. But what about me? Should I come along?"

"Well, it might be easier to get him to talk if it's just

one on one, don't you think? But I'd certainly feel a lot more comfortable if you were nearby, like maybe practicing your serve or something on another court?"

"Sure. Those courts are so far away from everything else, if *he* is the one who killed Lori, you don't want to be out there alone with him. I'll be your safety net. Or watchdog, or whatever." Dyna jumped up suddenly and pulled at Maggie's hand, her face eager. "Come on—let's go. Let's set you up for a lesson, then we can work out how you're going to pump him."

Maggie laughed and let Dyna pull her toward the hotel, her blond friend's ponytail—what remained of it—bouncing with each step. Maggie felt more subdued than Dyna, but she now had fewer qualms. She knew she would have gone ahead on her own if Dyna had refused to get involved. But it was so much better knowing someone would be there with you. Even if that someone was an animal-rights-activist-psychic-studying witch.

Once again Maggie walked the shaded pathway to the tennis courts alone, this time in fresh navy shorts and a loose, McHenry High School T-shirt. She and Dyna had decided to arrive separately.

"I get there a few minutes before your lesson—it's at two, right?—and just grab a basket of balls and an empty court and start practicing."

"Right. Now if we synchronize our watches . . ." Maggie grinned as Dyna looked at her watch. "Just kidding. No need to get too serious about this. After all, it'll probably lead nowhere." Maggie wondered, though, if she were trying to convince Dyna or herself. Deep down, she knew things might get *very* serious. Her brother Joe's face popped in her head and she winced, knowing just how he would react to this. 'What are you *doing* Maggie! I told you to get *out* of there.' Yes, he told her that, and she would, soon. As soon as she found out a few things, that is.

Her thoughts went back to yesterday, shortly after the police had taken charge of the murder scene. She remembered watching Rob as he lingered nearby, remembered noticing the intensity of his interest in all that was happening, an interest that somehow seemed detached and unemotional. She hoped to find out what that strong interest meant, among other things.

Maggie reached the path surrounding the courts and began to pass the one on which Dyna stood with an orange basket of balls, studiously ignoring Maggie as she went through the motions of practicing her toss and serve. Most balls flew wild, her thoughts apparently not on what she was doing. Suddenly there came the sounds of loud, angry shouting. Both women's heads snapped in the direction of the sports shop. The voice was Rob Clayton's.

"You jerk. You stupid—" They were spared the rest by the sound of a door slamming loudly. Muffled shouts still carried through, but were unintelligible. Something crashed against a wall.

Maggie caught Dyna's eye through the fence, and her face looked startled and bewildered. She shook her head and shrugged, indicating to Maggie she had no idea what was going on.

Maggie hesitated. She thought of getting closer to the sports shop to hear better, but then the shouting ended. She waited a moment, wondering what would happen next, if Rob would still show up for her lesson. She decided all she could do was go to her court and wait. She signaled to Dyna, pointing toward it—it was two courts farther down—and walked on. No other courts were occupied, and Maggie was doubly glad that Dyna would be lingering nearby.

She had uncovered her racquet and was trying some practice swings when she caught sight of Rob walking rapidly from the sports center. This could be a grim tennis

lesson, Maggie thought, and worse, a very uncommunica-
tive one. As he drew near, though, she was surprised to see
a calm expression on the tennis pro's face.

"Ready to attack that backhand?" he called as he looked
up and saw her watching him.

"Sure am," she called back lightly, but she wondered if
someone else with Rob Clayton's voice was back in the
center, shouting and throwing things, or if Rob had the
most amazing ability to switch emotions she had ever en-
countered. If he did, it was great from the cooling-down
side. What was he like in the flaring-up mode though? Did
he lose control as quickly as he seemed to gain it, become
violent enough in a moment, perhaps, to kill?

Maggie didn't have time to mull this over because Rob
hurried onto the court and got down to business right away.

"Let's see what you're doing now," he said. He set up
his ball basket near the net, and motioned her to stand at
the baseline. Then he began tossing balls for her to hit.

"Not bad, but this is what you're doing wrong." He dem-
onstrated with his own racquet, then went through the
proper motions of the backhand with her. He tossed more
balls at her, keeping up a constant patter of instruction, and
Maggie struggled to follow it all.

"Turn your shoulder more, that's right. Now follow
through—you didn't follow through on that one. See where
your ball ended up?"

She was swamped with detailed directions. She felt
clumsy and uncoordinated.

"Hey, that's a good one. Perfect!"

Maggie beamed. This was fun. She hit a few more. "I
think I'm starting to get the hang of it."

"Oops, you didn't step forward enough on that one. Always remember . . ." Back to square one.

The sun beat down on the court. Maggie wiped sweat
from her face and pushed back the short brown waves of

hair that were rapidly tightening into what Joe teasingly called, "little Shirley Temple curls."

"Do you think we could take a break?" Maggie finally asked, breaking into Rob's steady stream of instruction.

"Arm getting tired?" He glanced at Maggie and checked his watch. "Yeah, let's sit down awhile." He took her racquet from her, leaned it against the net, then led the way to a shaded bench beyond the fence. Maggie noticed he had barely worked up a sweat. His white tennis shorts and shirt still looked crisp and fresh, and the skin of his neck below the dark hair was tan and dry. She wrapped a towel around her own damp neck and dabbed at the edges of her hairline.

"Try to work on what you just learned," Rob said, "practicing until it feels natural, automatic." He filled a paper cup with water from a cooler and handed it to her, then filled one for himself.

"I don't know if it will ever feel natural." Maggie held the cold cup against her temple, then forehead and cheek. "I'm obviously not one of those natural athletes."

"Even a natural athlete has to work at it, and work hard."

"I guess you've played for a long time?" Maggie asked, glancing over.

"Since I was four," he grinned back at her, "and could barely hold a racquet."

"No kidding? Someone said you played at Wimbledon. Is that right?"

Rob's grin faded and he squinted at the sky. "Yeah, that's right. I had to qualify, but it was a dream come true. Something I spent years working toward. Did pretty good too, until, well, let's just say Wimbledon demands one hundred percent of its players, and suddenly I crashed down to about twenty-five percent."

"An injury?"

He gulped his water and threw the cup down, then picked it up again, tossing it into the nearby trash basket. "I don't like to talk about it much. I thought I was beginning a

career in the tournaments, and it didn't work out. That's
that." He raised an eyebrow as he turned and looked at her
with an easy smile. "I'd much rather talk about you. Heard
you're a teacher. That right?"

"Yes." Maggie heard his flirting tone now and felt annoyed. He seemed to be able to turn it on so easily. Was
he just trying to avoid talking about himself? She gave him
a cool look and said, "Math. High school."

"That's great."

"The math is great, but sometimes the system is less than
wonderful, like when they give me someone who hasn't
mastered multiplication yet and expect me to get him into
quadratic equations by the third quarter."

"Yeah, but isn't it great when you start to see some improvement and know you brought it about?"

Maggie looked at Rob, surprised. "Yes, it is. It's one of
the reasons I went into teaching." She took a sip a water.
Then, watching Rob's face closely, she said, "Did you
know that the girl whose body I found, Lori, was a student
of mine back in Baltimore?"

Rob looked back at her steadily, and she noticed a tightening at the side of his mouth. "I had heard that. I wasn't
sure it was true. Made it pretty tough, huh?"

"You could say that. Did you know her?"

His gaze moved in the general direction of the murder
scene. Bits of yellow tape from the investigation still clung
to a few trees. "Well, yeah, I know just about everyone
here. I ran into her now and then. Nice kid."

"She was. You didn't know her well, then?"

"No."

"Someone gave me the impression you two were seeing
each other."

"Your 'someone' doesn't know what they're talking
about."

Maggie shrugged. "Lori was a good kid. I had high

hopes for her when I taught her. I remember she enjoyed math. I wonder if she planned to do something with it?"

"Social work. I think. I mean, I think I heard someone say that's what she wanted."

"Mmm." A "nice kid" he ran into now and then whose college major he just happened to know. Maggie was sure he was holding back on her.

"So you didn't . . ." she began, but Rob suddenly jumped up from the bench and looked at his watch, scowling.

"Hey, I've got another lesson coming in a few minutes, but we could go over those backhand moves some more if you're up to it."

"Sure, why not." Maggie followed him back on the court, frustrated at having their talk cut short, but unable to come up with a way to extend it without tipping him off that he was being interrogated. This detective work was harder than she thought.

They repeated the same toss, swing, and critiques as before, and Maggie tried to concentrate, but her mind kept going back to their conversation. It wasn't enough. She should have kept him talking. She should have asked him where he was at the time Lori was killed. But he could easily lie about that, couldn't he? And how would she know?

She remembered how cool he was when she arrived for her match with Dyna yesterday. Would he have been so calm and casual if he had murdered someone a few hours earlier? But then, he had arrived for her lesson today looking quite calm, and she had heard him shouting and throwing things just minutes earlier. Maggie swung at a ball and missed.

"Your mind is wandering," Rob called. "That was an easy one."

"I'm sorry. I guess I'm getting tired."

"Our time is up anyway. Here comes my next lesson."

Maggie turned and saw a pair of energetic tow-headed

ten-year-olds, accompanied by a tired-looking mother, scrambling down the path.

"Hey Tyler! Hey Travis!" Rob greeted them with light boxing punches as they came onto the court, and they shrieked and giggled as they protected themselves. "Okay, you two, before we start I want to see three jogs around the court to warm up—next to the fence!"

The boys took off with noisy energy, and Maggie packed up her things.

Rob handed her her towel along with a few final words of advice. "You should practice alone before you play any games. If it doesn't get to be automatic, you'll just go right back to your old way of hitting."

She thanked him and promised to try. As she reached the gate she turned to watch for a moment. Rob had joined the twins in their run and they giggled at something he said. She smiled, but found herself wondering just who the *real* Rob Clayton was. There seemed to be a few sides to him that didn't quite fit together.

Maggie walked on down the path back to the sports center, her towel draped under her damp curls. She checked out the court Dyna had been on earlier, but her friend was nowhere to be seen. Did she leave already? Maggie looked around again, then walked over to the sports shop building. She glanced around inside from the doorway and saw no one at all.

"Did she think I had left when Rob and I were taking our time-out on the bench?" Maggie murmured to herself, puzzled.

She walked back out and started alone on the mulched path back to the hotel. She had gone about a hundred feet when she heard a stick crack somewhere behind her. She turned around and called, "Dyna?" No answer. Where *is* she, Maggie wondered, feeling annoyed now. She didn't like these woods any better than she had the first time, and decided to pick up her pace and get out into the open as soon as she could.

About another minute had gone by when she again heard the sound of someone stepping on dry sticks. She whirled around and called sharply, "Dyna, is that you? Who's there?"

At first there was silence. Then Maggie heard footsteps coming toward her, beyond the last curve in the path. A man in rumpled work clothes came into view. He walked lazily, hands in pockets, and wearing a grin that looked, to Maggie, more frightening than if he had been holding a weapon.

"Your girlfriend," he said as he came closer, "got held up."

Chapter Eleven

"Who are you?" Maggie tried to ask it with a measure of authority, as in, "Where is your hall pass?" or "Why aren't you in homeroom?" She took a deep breath and tried to hide the fear she actually felt.

The man grinned even more. "Don't matter, but I happen to work here." He pulled a hand out of his pocket and pointed to the Highview logo on his dark cotton shirt. On the pocket below was machine-stitched "Eric." He seemed to be in his mid-twenties, medium build, and might have been called good-looking with his even features and dark hair, except for a certain shifty-eyed sleaziness about him. He tilted his head to one side, looking at her teasingly, and said, "Saw you talking to ol' Rob back there."

"Yes?" Maggie watched him carefully. He hadn't made any threatening moves, but his manner was a long way from putting her at ease.

He pulled a toothpick out of his pocket and bit on it, moving it from side to side with his tongue, lizardlike, and

68

she relaxed some. Disgusting as the sight was, she somehow felt he was now less likely to make any aggressive
move toward her. Her grip on her racquet eased.

"Ol' Rob tell you all about his great tennis career?"

"Why?"

"Oh, I just wondered if he tried to snow you like he's
tried to snow all the others, that's all."

"Snow me?"

"Yeah," he grinned, and wiggled his fingers in a downward motion in the air, "snow, like that white stuff comes
outa the sky, or like—"

"Look, I've got to go." Maggie turned and started to
walk away. He fell into step with her and she knew there
was nothing she could do about it. But at least she was
moving.

"He tell you he got hurt at Wimbledon? And that's why
he don't play the tour no more?"

"What does it matter what he told me? Why do you
care?"

"Just trying to do a good deed." He grinned at her, catching the toothpick before it fell.

"Well, thanks anyway, but—"

"Truth is he got kicked off the tour. Dropped by his
coach. Like to guess why?"

"I'm sure you'd like to tell me."

"Beat up his girlfriend." He paused, then added with obvious satisfaction, "Yeah, that's right," when Maggie
turned a stunned face toward him.

When she didn't comment, he went on. "Got arrested
and everything, only the girlfriend decided not to press
charges and they had to let him go. Over there in England,
you know, this was."

"Is this true?" Maggie searched his face for credibility.
She had done the same to scores of teenaged boys trying
to get away with one thing or another at school. This face,
however, was harder to read.

"Sure it's true. The police couldn't hold him, but his coach knew what happened. The tournament guys knew. 'At's why he got kicked out. But he likes to tell his own story about it, make the girls feel so *sorry* for him. I just thought I'd save you some trouble." He went on grinning the whole time he talked, and Maggie was still unsure how seriously to take him. Was he making up a story to get back at Rob for some reason?

"Eric, before my lesson I heard Rob sounding pretty mad at someone. Was that you, by any chance?"

He looked down at her, his grin now reduced to a smirk, then took out his toothpick and studied it. Whether he was planning to answer her or not, Maggie never found out, because suddenly Dyna's voice came sailing down the path from around a bend.

"Maggie! Maggie, wait!"

"See you later," he said, then stepped off the path and disappeared into the trees.

"Maggie! There you are!" Dyna came to a stumbling halt as she caught sight of her friend. Her face was flushed and her hair flew out in several directions.

"Dyna! Where were you?"

"I got locked in!"

"Locked in where?"

"The rest room." Dyna put her hands on her knees and took several deep breaths. Then she flipped her hair out of her face and continued. "I saw those kids going with their mother for a lesson with Rob, so I knew you'd be okay for a while. I really *had* to go—all that water I drank 'cause it was so hot—so I ran over to the sports center and figured I'd be back before you were ready to leave."

"Well you weren't. I thought you had left without me."

"Maggie, I wouldn't do that!" Dyna looked so hurt that Maggie immediately regretted her angry tone.

"I'm sorry. I'm just jittery because of that creep." Maggie looked in the direction Eric had gone, but there was no sign of him.

"What creep? Who was here? Were you in trouble?"

Maggie told her about Eric, downplaying the fear she had felt at first and relating what he had told her about Rob.

"Oh my gosh. That sounds pretty bad. Is it true?"

"I don't know yet. Rob *was* evasive when I asked him about Wimbledon. But this Eric doesn't strike me as a sterling source of information. Maybe I can check it out." Maggie looked over at her friend. "But what about you? What did you mean about being locked in the rest room?"

"Maggie, it was weird." Dyna ran her fingers through her already wild hair. "I went into the sports shop to use the ladies' room, like I said. The door was kinda hard to pull open, like it was warped or something, you know? Anyway, I know I didn't pull it closed real tight, 'cause it wasn't a one-person rest room, but had stalls, so I didn't have to lock it or anything. So I'm sure I just pulled it closed enough to stay shut.

"Well, when I was drying my hands with one of those air driers, I thought I heard something, but I wasn't sure 'cause those things make such a noise right in your face, you know, blowing all that air. And when I tried to leave, I couldn't open the door! It was jammed shut, and I couldn't push it open!"

Maggie wasn't sure if she wanted to gasp or laugh from the picture Dyna was drawing her, but she asked, "How did you finally get out?"

"Well, after pushing and kicking at it and getting nowhere, I started hollering. Finally, these two guys walked into the shop, to get a court I guess, and heard me. They managed to pull the door open. Talk about embarrassing!"

"So it wasn't actually locked, then?"

"No, but just as good as."

"And you're sure you didn't pull it tight yourself?"

"Maggie, there was no way I could have done that. Honest. Besides, I was in a hurry, remember?"

Maggie smiled. "I know. I'm just trying to eliminate all other possibilities."

"All other possibilities except what?"

"That our friend Eric made sure you were, as he said, 'held up.' "

"But why? Why would he do such a thing? It seems such an adolescent kind of thing to do."

"Well, he didn't strike me as a model of maturity, but he might have wanted to make sure I was alone."

"Maggie!" Dyna looked at her, her eyes wide.

"To find me alone to talk to me, since that's what he did. But then, maybe he didn't think you'd be along so quickly. Maybe"—Maggie looked in the direction Eric had disappeared in the woods and rubbed the goose bumps that had formed on her arm—"just maybe he had other plans too."

Maggie and Dyna walked out of the woods, Dyna keeping up a steady stream of questions that Maggie couldn't answer, but which she knew must be coming from Dyna's store of nervous energy. Maggie still felt on edge herself.

As they walked across the expanse of lawn and came closer to the hotel, Maggie caught sight of a man dressed in the same kind of work uniform Eric had been. He was pruning a row of hedges. Maggie veered toward him and shushed Dyna's chatter with a raised hand.

"Just a sec. I want to ask this man something."

The workman looked over at their approach and nodded, but continued pruning.

"Excuse me," Maggie said as she came closer.

He lowered his shears and ran a hand through his thinning hair. He was tall and sinewy, probably in his forties, and he smiled a patient, polite smile.

"Yes, ma'am?"

"I just ran into a man near the tennis courts, about my age, dressed in a Highview uniform like yours with the name "Eric" stitched on the pocket. Do you happen to know him?"

"Was he chewin' on a toothpick?"

"Yes!"

"Then it's Eric Semple. He was s'posed to be doing the job I'm doing right now. So that's where he was."

The thick eyebrows on the man bunched together in an angry scowl. Maggie noticed the name on his pocket was "Jack."

"Was there any problem?" he asked.

"No, not really. It's just that running into anyone in those woods now can be unnerving. I wanted to make sure he really worked here."

"Well, he's been *hired*. Whether he actually *works* is something else. If management would let me hire my own workers I could get a damn sight more done around here. Well, anyway, yes Eric is *employed* here, but Miss, I'd keep my distance from him if I were you."

"Why is that?"

"Just keep your distance, that's all. Now, excuse me, I've got work to do." Jack picked up his pruning shears and walked away from Maggie and Dyna. He called out orders to another worker who was spreading mulch around newly planted shrubs. "Put it on a couple inches thicker, Cal." Then he turned into a clump of tall rhododendrons and disappeared.

Maggie and Dyna looked at each other.

"Well there go my plans for dinner and dancing tonight," Maggie deadpanned.

Dyna's jaw started to drop but then she grinned. "Jack sure has a low opinion of Eric, doesn't he?"

"Yes, which confirms my own impression. Let's get back to our rooms. Creep though he may be, we still don't know if Eric made up that whole story about Rob. If I can reach a certain person on the phone, I might be able to find out."

Back in her room Maggie took a quick shower, then placed a call to her friend Elizabeth Drury. Liz ran the school library at McHenry, and Maggie hoped she wouldn't mind doing a little research for her.

"Love to, Maggie," Liz sang out in her loud, nonlibrarian voice. "Here I thought all I'd be doing all summer is sending out overdue notices to the book thieves of McHenry High. You've made my day. Want to tell me what it's all about?"

"Can you wait on that, Liz? It might be important, or I might just be poking into someone's private business. I don't know yet."

"Ooh, how mysterious. Maggie Olenski, private eye. Well, give me those names and dates and I'll see what I can come up with."

"Thanks a million, Liz. Next time you need figures checked for your budget report, I'm your woman." She gave Liz the pertinent information and hung up, crossing her fingers that the librarian would have good luck.

She was still looking at the phone thoughtfully when she heard a soft knock on her door. Maggie walked over, but instead of immediately opening the door as she normally would have, she peeked cautiously through the peephole. It was Holly, the waitress she had talked with at the bar. Maggie lifted the chain and let her in.

"Hi. I saw you come back. I've been waiting to give you something." Holly held out a slim, black hardcover book, about six by ten inches. She seemed uneasy.

"What is it?" Maggie asked, taking it from her.

"It's Lori's. She used to write in it once in a while, when things were slow. I found it in the kitchen, mixed in with some trays. She must have put it there in a hurry one time, and it got shoved back." Holly put a fingernail to her teeth and began to nibble.

"Holly, you should give this to the sheriff. This could be very important."

"I know. But, I thought maybe you could give it to him? You seem kinda involved in this, what with knowing Lori and finding her body and all. I mean, you *care* about her, so you'll see something is done about this. That's why I'm not just passing it on to someone here. And I could give it to the sheriff, but"—Holly looked at her with a crooked smile—"well, I'd just as soon keep my distance, if you know what I mean. There was something, well, it was years ago and it was just stupid trouble kids get into, you know, but still. . . ."

"Well, sure, then. I'll take it to him."

"Thanks." Holly looked relieved and turned to leave.

"Can you stay a minute? There's a couple things I'd like to ask you."

Holly looked at her watch and shrugged. "I've got some time, I guess, before old Crawford sends someone looking for me."

"Good. I was wondering how long Rob has been here at the hotel. Do you know?"

"Working here? Jeez, let me see. I've been here two years. He was here when I came, and I think he had started about three months before that. Yeah, I remember someone telling me he came in March for the spring season."

"And that girl you told me about? She died when?"

"September, that year."

"So Rob would have known her?"

"Yeah." Holly looked at her curiously. "Why?"

"Do you think he knew her well? I'm wondering if there could have been any connection between Rob and this girl's death."

"Ohmigosh! Rob? No, there couldn't have been any connection. She was going with some other guy. Remember, I said she was going to get married?" Holly frowned. "But now that I think of it . . ."

"Yes? What?"

"Well, it's not that much of a connection, but she did play tennis once in a while. She might have taken lessons. I don't know for sure. But they said she died from an overdose of pills. She wouldn't have done that over a bad serve!"

"Of course not. But you said you didn't believe she killed herself, didn't you? If not, someone else did."

"You think Rob did?"

"I don't think anything yet. I'm just asking questions. And please don't mention this to anyone, okay? I don't want to start rumors."

"Yeah, sure. But how about I ask around a little, see if anyone else knows if Rob had much to do with her?"

"That'd be great, but do it as quietly as you can. Oh, one other thing," Maggie put her hand on the younger woman's arm as she turned toward the door. "I met someone on the grounds today who works here. His name is Eric. Do you know him?"

"Eric Semple? Dark hair, not bad-looking, about this tall?" Holly held her hand several inches above her head.

Maggie nodded.

"Sure, I know him. Works in maintenance." Holly glanced at her watch and opened Maggie's door, looking out carefully in both directions. "He's okay." She stepped out, then grinned. "Kind of a goof-off. He got his job here, of course, because he's *her* son."

"Her? Who do you mean?"

"Burnelle. You know. I saw her come up here. The housekeeping supervisor who brought your dinner that first night." Holly lifted her hand in farewell, grinned, and scurried down the hall.

Chapter Twelve

Maggie stood and stared down the hallway after Holly, then closed the door. Eric Semple, that sleazy, toothpick-chewer who trapped women in rest rooms, was related to Burnelle, the friendly, conscientious housekeeper who disapproved of young ladies touching alcohol? And not just related, but her *son*? Maggie's mind grappled with the concept.

Her immediate reaction was a feeling of sympathy for the woman. She was obviously hardworking and self-disciplined. Apparently Burnelle had been instrumental in getting Eric his job here. That might be what Jack, the gardener, referred to when he complained about his lack of control in hiring helpers.

Maggie wondered how many other jobs Eric might have gone through before coming to work at the same place as his mother. The two just didn't fit together. It was like trying to imagine Clara Barton as the mother of Billy the Kid.

Maggie's thoughts turned to her own mother, to their own relationship. Who would someone compare them to? They were certainly two very different people, from different worlds, who sometimes spoke the same words that often came out with opposite meanings. Human offspring obviously were not clones of their parents. At least not yet.

Maggie shook her head, then remembered the book Holly had brought, which she still held in her hands. She knew that legally she should immediately turn it over to the authorities. But there might be much she could learn from it. Surely it wouldn't matter waiting a few hours? Having rationalized the situation to her satisfaction, Maggie opened it up and started to read, walking over to the soft chair near the window of her room and sinking slowly into it.

The book was lined and columned, an accounting-type notebook that Lori had apparently decided to use as her personal journal. The first few pages were filled with poems copied in longhand. Maggie recognized one or two from the high school English curriculum. Mac, her office partner, had quoted them often enough for them to stick in her memory.

These were followed by what seemed to be Lori's attempt at writing poetry. Many words and whole lines had been crossed out, but Maggie could piece them together well enough. They were the usual romantic, idealistic thoughts of a young college girl, but one or two lines touched Maggie. She could see how Lori had matured from the fifteen-year-old she had once tutored.

The poetry changed to prose. Lori began putting down her thoughts, apparently near the end of her last semester in college. Random and unconnected, they appeared to have been written quickly.

Wish I had spent more time on philosophy—it's just starting to click and I really like it now. Is it too late?

Steph wants to fix me up with her boyfriend's brother for Saturday night. I told her no and I'm afraid she's a little mad. I wish people would stop trying to fix me up. I just can't seem to get interested in any of the guys I've met so far. I don't know why, exactly. They just seem so young.

Soon came comments on starting work at the Highview. Maggie read about Lori's excitement at getting the job, then her anxiety just before starting. Lori mentioned the names of a few of the other waitresses—including Holly—and wrote about the brief training period. Maggie flipped pages until she came to the last entry. There was no date, and no indication—to Maggie's disappointment—that Lori planned to meet someone. The final note could have been written on her last day of life or weeks earlier.

We talked again today. He seemed pretty down, and I couldn't shake him out of it. I really wish I could help, but I'm racking my brains and can't figure out how yet. Maybe just moral support. He needs to make the change.

Maggie's breath quickened, and she searched several of the preceeding pages for a name to connect with "him." She found nothing. Suddenly the phone rang, and Maggie jumped up and grabbed it.

"Maggie?"

"Uh-huh."

"It's me, Dyna. Are you okay? You sound funny."

"I'm all right, Dyna. I was just reading something. What's up?"

"I wanted to tell you to go on to dinner without me. I've got a rotten headache, so I'm going to hang around here the rest of the night."

"That's too bad. Can I get you something for it?"

"No, I avoid medications whenever possible. I'm just going to do some deep breathing excercises, some chanting, and try to meditate."

Maggie smiled, thinking that popping a simple aspirin might save a whole lot of time and effort, then shrugged. Whatever works.

"I hope you feel better, Dyna. Maybe being out in that hot sun today brought it on."

"Yeah, maybe. I think letting myself get so shook up in the ladies' room kinda upset my aura, too. That's why I need to calm it down."

Time to hang up. "Well, good luck. I'll see you in the morning." Maggie put down the phone and looked out the window. Dyna's mention of dinner had surprised her. She hadn't realized it was getting so late. But the long shadows outside, as well as the empty feeling in her stomach, convinced her.

She opened her suitcase and slipped the black book in, then locked it. She glanced in the mirror and decided that the walking shorts and blouse she had on would do. The Highview was not a dress-for-dinner kind of place. A touch of lipstick and a quick fluff of her hair with the brush, and she was soon out her door, locking it behind her.

Maggie looked around the dining room, which was pleasantly decorated in shades of tan and amber, with framed watercolors on the walls and soft lighting; she chose a small table next to the window. Only a few scattered tables still had diners. She was studying the menu when a voice interrupted her. A thin, middle-aged woman had stopped beside her.

"Hello, dear. How *are* you?" The question was clearly more than just a polite greeting, and Maggie recognized the woman who had been practicing on the next court when they found Lori. She had a look of motherly concern on her face. Maggie smiled.

"I'm fine, thanks. It's nice to see you."

The woman introduced herself and the man who now stood beside her as Charlotte and Don McManus.

"I wish I had known you were going to dine here tonight. We would have been so glad for you to join us," she said.

"Thanks, that would have been great, but I'm okay, really," Maggie said. But after they left, she was more conscious of her aloneness. She ordered dinner, then, needing to do something other than gaze at the walls or the other diners, pulled out paper and a pencil and started doodling. She soon found herself sketching a small square, dividing it into nine parts, and filling it slowly with numbers. The idea was to make a "magic" square, a square with differing numbers whose total in any direction—including diagonal, if you were good—was always the same.

As she worked, her mother's voice crept into her head, exclaiming, as she often did, over Maggie's curious pastimes. "Where you got your head for numbers, I don't know. Your father and I need the calculator for anything at the bakery, and we still sometimes mess up." Then a warning followed, one that Maggie had heard many times and which still irritated her. "Don't let your boyfriends see you doing that. You'll scare them away."

Maggie knew her mother only echoed attitudes that had been drummed into her as a girl. "Don't seem too smart. Let the man do all the talking. Hang on his every word." Maggie felt she was enough of a woman of her own generation to let most of that just roll off of her. But it still grated. She wished her mother could just be proud of her daughter's intelligence instead of worrying that it somehow made her unapproachable.

She put down her pencil and gazed out the windows at the pretty flower-lined walkway. The sun had sunk more than halfway behind the mountain peaks, throwing the area into shadows. Small lights began to blink on, and a young couple strolled by, holding hands.

Maggie smiled at the peaceful beauty of it and, watching

the couple, found herself trying to remember when her last date had been. *Did* she come across as too smart for most men? Did she not let them do enough of the talking? Maggie shook her head firmly. She wasn't going to let herself fall into that trap.

"You don't approve of the landscaping?"

Maggie started and looked up. Rob Clayton stood beside her table, wearing a casual shirt and slacks, and a wry smile. "I told them," he said, "don't put the peonies next to the lariope, but would they listen?"

Maggie laughed. "I think it all looks perfectly lovely. My thoughts had been wandering to something else." She felt a twinge of embarrassment and, annoyed with herself, immediately squelched it.

"You looked like you could use someone to share your thoughts with. There's nothing worse than eating alone in a room full of other people talking to each other, don't you think?"

"Absolutely. And I think it'd be great if you would join me. That is, if you haven't eaten yet?"

"As a matter of fact I have, except for dessert. So if you don't mind seeing me pig out on pecan pie, then I will join you. I hate eating alone too." Rob pulled out the chair opposite her, and caught the waitress's eye. She brought over his dessert and coffee and, before long, Maggie's order of baked salmon.

Maggie pushed aside her "magic square" doodle, but purposely left it out in plain sight, thinking to herself with an inner smile that her mother would *not* approve. She couldn't help wondering why Rob was alone. Surely an attractive man like him . . . She stopped that thought. This was another chance for her to find out more about his connection with Lori, and she needed to concentrate on that.

"Hope I didn't overwork you at the lesson today," Rob said, as Maggie slid her fork into her entree.

She shook her head. "I'm just so out of condition. The

workout was good for me. And I could definitely see my backhand improving. Now if I can only remember what I learned, I just might be able to play a decent game of tennis."

"You've a got a decent game already. Now you can bring it up to a challenging one. And you'll have more fun with it."

Maggie's thoughts jumped to her encounter with Eric Semple after the lesson and the things he had said about Rob. Should she bring it up? She felt reluctant to spoil the pleasant mood. Maybe later.

"This isn't your first job as a tennis director, is it?" she asked.

"No, I've been at a few resorts like this. The last one was up in Pennsylvania. But when this became available, I took it. It was a step up, and I like this area. Grew up not too far from here, as a matter of fact."

"Really? So you have family nearby?"

"Well, my mother. She owns a small business in Hagerstown."

"You said you started playing tennis at four. Was she a player?"

Rob laughed. "No. Wherever I got my ability for the game, it wasn't from her."

He didn't mention his father, Maggie noticed. Not in the picture?

"But there were courts nearby where we lived, in the park where Mom used to take me. The guy who was giving tennis lessons there took a shine to me, and I took a shine to the game. It just grew from there. Mom worked hard to get me private lessons and send me to tennis camps as I grew up, second jobs waitressing, and all. She sacrificed a lot." Rob's face had grown serious, and as if he realized it, he suddenly grinned. "Enough about me, though. Tell me about you."

"There's not much to tell," Maggie said. She took a sip

of water. "I'm from Baltimore. Or rather, just outside it. My folks have a bakery, and my brother Joe and I helped out in it. Since it was open six days a week, it took up a lot of our time. It probably taught us a lot, but the main thing I seemed to get out of it was a determination never to go into a business of my own. It can be all-consuming. You never get away from it."

"But you had all the cookies you could eat?"

Maggie laughed. "That I did. And even though working behind the counter was often tedious, our customers were always in a good mood as they picked out their confection for the day. I remember one summer, though, a weight-loss center opened up right next door to us. A bad choice of location. They lasted one season, then packed up and moved somewhere else. We were apparently very bad for their clients' willpower."

Rob grinned. "So you went into teaching instead of baking."

"I chose math, actually, then later decided to teach it. It's been a good decision, so far." She thought of Rob's comfortable manner at the tennis lesson. "You have quite a knack for teaching yourself. I learned a lot, and those two little boys whose lesson was right after mine certainly seemed to enjoy it."

"Tyler and Travis? Yeah." He grinned. "They're great kids."

"They're how old—about ten? How do you manage to make something like tennis fun for kids that age? I would think they'd get bored with all the practice required."

"Ah, that's the trick." Rob put down the coffee cup he had raised halfway to his mouth and looked at Maggie, his face animated. "You make a game of every part of it, changing the game constantly while still repeating the motions they're going through. They think they're doing something different all the time. Like when they're learning to serve. . . ."

Rob launched into a detailed description of some of the things he had the twins go through, his expression eager as he told of the successes of some of his strategies, and humorously self-deprecating as he told of the failures. "They keep me on my toes the whole time," he assured her.

Maggie listened with fascination, less with the subject than at the change she saw come over the speaker. A kind of glow of enthusiasm emanated from him. Rob had many sides to him, that she had noticed before, and this definitely was one of the nicer ones.

"You seem to really enjoy working with kids," she said when he finished.

His smile became a bit embarrassed, and he looked down at his plate, scraping the last crumbs of his pecan pie together with his fork. "Yeah, I do."

Could someone like this ever actually beat up a girlfriend? Or maybe worse? Maggie struggled with the thought.

"And I think I'm good at it," Rob said. "In fact—" He paused and looked out the window, as though deciding whether to say more, then turned back to Maggie. "I have a dream of having my own tennis camp for kids someday." He seemed to wait for her reaction before saying more.

"Really? What a great idea," Maggie said, meaning it sincerely on one level, but conscious of an uneasiness on another. There were still too many questions in her mind about this man.

He seemed to grab at the enthusiasm in her voice, though, and launched into a description of what he had in mind. "Of course, this all depends on a lot of things—major things. Financial backing for one."

"I have a feeling you'll work it out," Maggie said. "When people want something badly enough, they usually find a way to get it." She added with a smile, "I can't help thinking of that old Chinese proverb, though. 'Be careful what you wish for. You just might get it.' "

Rob laughed. "I know. Like, I might find myself some-day surrounded by whining, screaming, snot-nosed kids, and wondering how the hell to get out of it all."

"Something like that."

"Well, however it turns out, at least it couldn't be much worse than working here has been sometimes." He glanced around. "Strictly between you and me, of course."

Maggie's eyebrows arched up.

Rob nodded, his face grim. "Some of the things I've had to put up with. If it weren't for the money...."

Maggie had heard that same phrase before, from Holly. She knew it wasn't highly unusual for employees to complain about their jobs. Any lunchtime in the teachers' lounge back at McHenry she was bound to hear a grumble or two. But there was something about the way he said this—"If it weren't for the money...." His tone and the expression on his face implied deeper problems than she could guess at.

Maggie thought of the angry shouting she had heard just before her lesson that afternoon. It could have been a result of the problems Rob had to deal with here, or it could have risen from a nasty temper. She didn't know which. She decided to try to find out.

"Um, I happened to talk to one of the maintenance workers today, a guy named Eric."

Rob's face darkened. "He's one of the things I'm talking about. The guy's supposed to do certain jobs for me, but he's completely undependable. He's a real loser. Lies as easily as breathing. And worse. I'd keep away from him if I were you."

"Oh?" This was the second time Maggie had been told to keep her distance from Eric. But she wondered why Rob felt the need to label Eric a liar. Did he suspect Eric had been talking about him?

"If it weren't for his mother, he'd be out of here so fast

. . . well, never mind. I won't bore you with our staff problems."

"Oh, I don't mind. I just found out a little while ago that Eric's mother is Burnelle, the housekeeping supervisor. I could hardly believe it. So she is able to keep him working here, even though he's incompetent?"

"Yeah. Management seems to think a lot of her. I heard they brought her here from another hotel of theirs. Maybe they're afraid they'll lose her if they fire him, and figure they can survive one low-level no-good for a while."

"Was he the one you were yelling at just before my lesson?"

Rob eyebrows shot up in surprise. Then he grinned at her. "You heard? Yeah, probably everyone within a half-mile heard. The guy just . . . Well, never mind." He looked at her empty plate, then back up at her. "Ready for dessert? Coffee? Or maybe an after-dinner drink?"

Maggie decided not to ask Rob about what Eric had said about Wimbledon. Not yet. She'd wait and see what Liz could find out for her. She shook her head at the food and drink suggestions.

"This dinner was huge, and as you can see, I polished it off. I think I'd better quit now." Maggie pictured Lori's notebook locked in her suitcase upstairs. She was eager to get back to it. "I have some things to do tonight before I turn in," she said. "Thanks for the company. I enjoyed it."

He rose as she did, and seemed on the verge of suggesting an extension to the evening, or at least leaving with her, but she walked off quickly before he had the chance. As she waited for the elevator she thought about her last comment. She *had* enjoyed it—dinner with someone whom she considered a possible murder suspect. Could he possibly know she considered him that? And was he, perhaps, purposely charming her? For now, she could only wonder.

She jabbed at the elevator button a second time. Something seemed to be holding it up on two. As she gazed up at the elevator lights, an angry voice nearby caught her attention. Maggie turned and saw a fairly young woman whose air of cold disapproval and severe hairstyle aged her. She was reprimanding the night deskman, who cowered at her words.

"When are you going to learn this phone system?" she scolded, like an angry schoolmarm. "I've gone over and over it with you. Yesterday you lost a call for me, and now you've lost a return call from the sheriff for my mother. She may not be able to reach him again."

"I'm sorry, Miss Crawford."

Miss Crawford. So that must be Kathryn Crawford's daughter, whom Holly seemed to dislike. Maggie could see why. Not a pleasant person, at least where the hotel employees were concerned. She turned back to face the elevator, still hearing the young woman going over the intricacies of the phone with exaggerated patience, as though speaking to someone who was mentally challenged. The elevator doors opened and Maggie stepped in, punched in her floor button, and waited as the doors slowly closed.

So Kathryn Crawford had a return call from the sheriff, she thought, as the elevator hummed and glided smoothly upward. Did it have something to do with Lori's murder? Why would the Highview manager be calling the sheriff this late in the evening? Maggie wished she could be a fly and perch on the woman's office wall for a while. What interesting things might she learn?

Back in her room Maggie retrieved Lori's black book and curled up on the bed to read it. She thought of calling Dyna first, to see how she was feeling, but decided she'd either interrupt sleep or meditations. She turned to the section that dealt with Lori's work at the Highview.

Made a real mess today—my first day on the job! I piled too many things on my tray, and it started tipping, and the coffee sloshed all over the scrambled eggs! Holly showed me how to do it better. She makes it all look so easy.

Burnelle stopped me as I was leaving and said I did real well for a first day. That was so nice of her. That made me made me feel good, especially after getting the evil eye from Ms. Crawford anytime I passed by. I felt she was watching me, and that made me more nervous.

Lori described a few more problems with learning her job, and then things apparently smoothed out and she moved on to other concerns. She wrote about working with the local blood drive and encouraging her co-workers to donate.

Everyone was so great about it! Mostly I helped keep the paperwork straight. They kept me busy but it was a lot of fun. <u>Nobody</u> fainted, which I heard was a kind of record!

Maggie remembered when Lori was back at McHenry High. She volunteered for a fundraising flea market to buy new uniforms for the band, even though she wasn't in the band. When Maggie asked why she was doing it, Lori laughed and said she just liked helping out. Even at fifteen Lori showed a quiet kind of leadership, the kind that got things done without a lot of fanfare. Maggie sighed, and read on.

Lori mentioned Eric in her jottings, and the fact that he was Burnelle's son. Lori sensed he was unhappy with his job, that he disliked grounds' maintenance. She wondered if he stayed on only for his mother's sake.

I know Burnelle is only trying to do her best for him. But I think he'd be happier doing something else. Maybe he should go back to school? But there's always the problem of money.

She mentioned meeting Rob Clayton.

Ran into that cute tennis instructor—literally. I was hurrying to work from the parking lot and ran right into him as I rounded the corner. He helped me pick up my things and carried them into the kitchen for me. I got teased by the girls about it—they think he's pretty flirty. But I think he was just being nice.

As the pages filled, Lori began to use only initials for names.

H. and J. asked me to go out with them tonight after work. I said no. Hope I didn't sound rude.

B. got upset when H. didn't sign out like she should have. Sometimes I think H. does things on purpose, just to see what B. will do. She doesn't seem to like her. I don't understand why.

Then:

Dragged out my science book. It's amazing how much stuff I forgot. The girls think I'm weird looking through books like that, instead of something like a romance book. More teasing.

So that must be why she had the science book, Maggie said to herself. Was it the same one that was found with her body?

Maggie read through the next few pages, then came upon an entry that made her heart jump.

Saw R. again today. He seemed so down. All I can do is listen for now. Is that enough? I wish I could do more.

Chapter Thirteen

Maggie was dancing with Rob. She wore a gauzy, flowing gown, and they floated around the dance floor. Suddenly Rob became Eric Semple, grinning at her and holding on to her tightly as she tried to pull away. The music played faster, and she struggled to keep from stumbling. She looked around desperately for Rob, hoping for rescue, and finally saw him dancing with someone else off in the distance. As they turned their faces toward her, she saw it was Lori. They both threw back their heads, laughing, then whirled away, disappearing together. . . .

"No!" Maggie called, reaching out, then realized she was in her bed at the Highview. Her heart beat rapidly, and she took several deep breaths, gradually calming down. "Wow," she said, running her hands through her hair and shaking her head to clear it. "Where did all that come from?" She rarely had upsetting dreams, and she was surprised at her reaction to this one. Was it because Lori had been in it? Or Rob?

She swung her legs over the edge of the bed, determined not to let the dream bother her any more. It was probably brought on simply from something she ate. She had a busy morning ahead of her, and needed a clear head, not one distracted by silly dreams. And that's all it was, a silly dream. But she couldn't rid herself of the uneasy feeling the dream had forced on her, try as she might to think of other things, occupying herself with getting ready for her day.

She had showered and dressed when she heard a knock on the door. A peek through the peephole showed Burnelle standing there with a cleaning cart. Maggie opened the door.

"Good morning," Burnelle said. "If you're leaving for breakfast, I could do your room. We're still a little short-handed, and I'm trying to help keep things on schedule."

"Sure. Come on in. I'll be leaving in a minute." Maggie held the door for her, then walked to the phone. She punched in Dyna's number and was glad to hear a lively hello.

"Dyna, it's me. Feeling better? Want to meet for breakfast?"

"Yeah, great. I was just going to call you. How about the terrace in five minutes?"

"Sounds good."

"Any plans for later?" Dyna asked.

"Yes, I have to go somewhere, but I'll tell you about it downstairs. See you." Maggie hung up the phone and turned to see Burnelle waiting patiently by the bed. Lori's book as well as Maggie's purse were on it. "Oh," Maggie said, "let me get these out of your way." Maggie felt stupid for having left the book in plain sight. She was starting to feel nervous about still having it, and the fewer people that were aware of it the better.

"Take your time, dear," Burnelle said. "You keep a diary?" she asked, nodding toward the black book. She began pulling off the bedclothes.

"No," Maggie said, evading an explanation. It was possible Holly could get in trouble for having given it to her. "But I do jot things down now and then so I don't forget them."

"Lots of people do that. Lots of famous people kept diaries." She shook a pillow out of its case. "John Brown for one. You heard of him?"

Maggie nodded. She was checking her purse for car keys and other essentials. She would go to the sheriff's right after breakfast.

"I guess everyone's heard of him. A lot's been written about him. A lot of mistaken things. But he kept his own diary. It's there in the museum in my hometown. It explains what he was trying to do. I took my son to that museum many a time when he was little."

Maggie turned. "Eric?"

"Yes." Burnelle looked up, pleased. "You've met my son?"

"Yes, I ran into him yesterday afternoon. Near the tennis courts." Maggie tried her best to smile as she said it.

Burnelle beamed. "Working hard, I'm sure. I'm so proud of him. He had his problems growing up, like most boys do, but he's settled down so nicely now. He's anxious to do well here. And he will. He's a very bright boy, and he tries hard. But I sometimes worry that he might overdo it. I try to keep an eye on him, watch out for him, without, you know, letting him know." She walked back to her cart in the hall and came back with an armful of clean linen.

Maggie wondered at the degree of self-delusion that maternal love could bring about. She had seen it in certain parents at school. Johnny was going to be the next president of the United States, despite the fact that he was flunking nearly all his classes, and oh yes, that little arrest for drug use. But never mind all that. Burnelle seemed to be that kind of mother, and Maggie could only feel sorry for her.

Maggie slid the strap of her purse onto her shoulder, then tucked the journal under her arm. "Well, I'll be on my way."

Burnelle nodded and gazed at Maggie with a faraway look, still thinking perhaps of her beloved son. "Enjoy your breakfast," she said, then turned and flapped a clean white sheet over the bed.

Maggie pushed through the glass doors of the lobby and stepped onto the terrace. Warm, humid air hit her face, foretelling another hot day, but the patio, facing west, was still comfortably shaded. Round umbrella-topped tables dotted the slate flooring, and the pleasant aroma of fresh coffee wafted through the air. Maggie looked around, then saw Dyna sipping orange juice at an isolated table next to tall green hedges.

Dyna saw her and waved, and Maggie walked over, pulling out a chair to sit across from her. "Well, you look like you slept well."

"Mmm." Dyna nodded. "Like a rock. Everything's back in balance again."

"I'm glad. Did you order yet?"

"Just juice and coffee." Dyna indicated the two carafes on their table. Maggie reached for the coffee and poured out a steaming cupful for herself. She knew by now that Dyna would stick with juice alone, spurning the less healthy caffeine.

After the waiter took their orders, Maggie sat back in her chair and took a long sip from her cup. Dyna glanced over at the nearby pool, its blue water now empty and calm.

"This makes me think of a vacation I went on with my folks once—to Jamaica."

"Really? What about the Highview reminds you of Jamaica?"

"Well, there's a mountain area there—I forget what it's called. Port Something-or-other. Anyway, the other side of the island from Montego Bay. We stayed at this place that had tables out like this, and mountains around us. It was really pretty. More flowers than here, though. Big, bright ones."

"Sounds nice."

"Mmm, it was." Dyna stretched her arms above her head, then ran her fingers through her hair, apparently unconcerned with how she rearranged it. She wore yellow and white today in the shape of an oversized shirt and snug shorts, with a few chains of colored beads hanging over the shirt.

"I was eighteen then, and I remember Dad was trying to convince me to try college. 'Just for a year,' I remember him saying. I guess he hoped once I started I'd be hooked or something. He almost had me convinced, too. I mean, I didn't know what else to do with myself at that time."

At *that* time? Maggie was tempted to tease, but held her tongue.

"But then we went down to Kingston to look around the shops and stuff. That's where I found this most amazing woman. She not only could tell me all about myself—things she couldn't have *ever* known—she told me about my *past* lives too. It was like she could look right into my soul, you know?"

Maggie didn't know, but she nodded, thinking that her friend certainly made interesting early morning conversation.

Dyna leaned back in her chair. "Well, after an experience like that, there was no way I was going to sit in class to study the usual earthbound, mundane things. That's when I knew I wanted to find out all about witchcraft—the good kind—and paranormal things. There's a place up in New Hampshire, a school you can go to. Did you know that?"

"No, I didn't."

Dyna exhaled heavily, blowing wispy bangs up off her forehead. "I went there and I tried, I really did. But sometimes you have to admit you just don't have a talent for something, no matter how badly you want to do it."

Maggie wasn't sure if she should offer sympathy or congratulations. But since their food arrived at that time, she simply offered a bagel. Dyna brightened immediately and reached for it, her career woes quickly forgotten.

Maggie glanced down at the plate in front of her and called the waiter back. "I'm afraid you brought me the wrong order. I asked for the eggs well done, not sunny side up." Maggie looked at the two soft, yellow yolks jiggling on top of the eggs and stifled a shudder.

"Oh, gosh, I'm sorry!" The young waiter looked embarrassed and apologized as he took Maggie's plate away, rushing back to the kitchen.

"He's new, isn't he?" Dyna asked as she watched him go. "Maybe they hired him to replace Lori, 'cause I don't think I've seen him before."

The waiter, whose nametag, Maggie noticed, said "Chuck," brought the correct order to the table and apologized again for the mistake. He was tall and broad-shouldered, with sandy hair that fell over his forehead. She also noticed his hands were shaking as he set the plate down, and she smiled at him reassuringly. It was tough, she knew, breaking in on a new job.

She put her fork into her new eggs and nodded with satisfaction as it hit solid yolk. Old habits die hard, she thought, aware that the only reason she couldn't bear soft eggs was because her brother, Joe, had once compared them to something particularly disgusting back at the age of seven, turning her off them forever.

"You know," Maggie said, "it's interesting that you said your folks were eager for you to go to college. Mine, I think, would have been delighted if I'd stayed home after high school and just worked in the bakery with them."

"Yeah?"

"Mom, especially. I think it was fear of the unknown. She'd been kept close to home by my grandparents, who were immigrants, and college must have been a strange, scary world to her, a place she didn't want to put her daughter into. If it weren't for the partial scholarship I won, and my high school counselor urging them to send me, I might not have gone, or at least I would have had a much harder time of it. Even then, they insisted I live at home and commute."

"That's funny. It's like we were both born into the wrong set of parents. Maybe we were switched at birth, or should have been."

Maggie wondered how her conservative parents would have enjoyed having a daughter interested in witchcraft, and her lips twitched at the thought. She turned back to her food, scooping up the last of her eggs and munching quietly on her bagel. When she reached the point of her second cup of coffee, Maggie held up Lori's journal to show Dyna. She explained what it was and how she got it.

"You've read it?" Dyna asked.

"Yes. Unfortunately Lori's privacy doesn't exist anymore, and if I gave it to the sheriff unread, who knows how long it might languish in a drawer before anyone did anything about it."

"Yeah. So what did you find out from it?"

Maggie let out a sigh. "Not a whole lot, I'm afraid. She writes about things that happened here, but after a while she goes into a kind of shorthand, using initials instead of names. And she doesn't give full details of an incident. But then, she wasn't writing for anyone but herself, and *she* knew what she was writing about."

"Bummer." Dyna took a final bite of bagel.

Maggie nodded. "It's frustrating."

"So it's not any help?"

"Well, some." Maggie told Dyna about the entry mentioning "R."

"R," Dyna said, her brow wrinkling. "Do you think she means Rob?"

"I don't know. She could." Maggie frowned. She realized she didn't want it to mean Rob, but hated to admit it. She looked at Dyna. "I had dinner with him last night."

"With Rob?"

Maggie nodded.

"Did you find out anything more?"

"Well, I found out he has a low opinion of Eric Semple, the guy who came up to me on the path yesterday. He was the one we heard Rob shouting at." Maggie paused, then added with a smile. "I also found out he likes kids a lot. He'd like to have his own tennis camp someday."

Dyna looked at her friend for a moment, tilting her head. "Hey, are you falling for this guy?"

"No!" Maggie answered too quickly, then repeated again a more controlled "no. It just happens that there's a rather nice side to him. If it turns out he killed Lori, of course, that wouldn't matter. That would cancel everything out. But I'm just trying to keep an open mind. Innocent until proven guilty, you know. I'm trying to be logical."

"Right, 'cause that's what you're good at—logic. I mean, with your math and all."

Maggie nodded, but her mind wandered to the image of Rob sitting across from her at the table last night, his blue shirt picking up the blue in his eyes. The image lingered there for just a moment, until she returned back to the present. Logic, yes, logic.

Chuck came back to their table, and they waited in silence as he began to clear the dishes. Suddenly though, while reaching for something, he knocked a water glass over. Maggie quickly grabbed at Lori's journal to keep it from getting soaked.

"I'm sorry. I'm really sorry," he apologized. He was at

least getting good at that. His ears reddened and he looked flustered. "Did I get your book wet?"

Maggie shook her head. "No, it's okay."

He mopped up the water with more stammerings, then escaped a final time to the kitchen.

"I think you're right," Maggie said with a smile after he had gone. "He must be new." She gathered up her things and stood up. "I'd better get this over to the sheriff's. Want to come?"

Dyna wrinkled her nose. "No thanks. I think I'll hang around here. I might join the aerobics class at ten."

"Okay. I'll see you later then." Maggie stood up, gathering her things, and caught sight of their young waiter at the back of the patio. He was saying something to Kathryn Crawford, who looked her usual grim self, and whose gaze was aimed over his shoulder directly at Maggie. Had she seen his accident? Maggie wondered. Was she chewing him out about it? He, however, seemed to be doing all the talking.

Maggie turned to leave, but before she could take a step, a small-sized head and shoulder suddenly bumped her sharply from behind. She nearly lost her balance and grabbed onto the table.

"Oh, sorry!" Tyler, one of the twins from the tennis courts, stood before her, gasping, but the look on his face showed he assumed she would think it was just as much fun as he did. He picked up Lori's book for her, which had fallen to the slate, then ran on his way. His laughing twin brother soon followed, and Maggie quickly stepped out of the way.

Before she had time to catch her breath, Rob Clayton appeared from behind the hedge. "Where did those two delinquents go?" he asked her. He tried to look severe, but he obviously was enjoying himself as much as the boys.

"They went that-a-way," Maggie said, pointing to the other corner of the hedge leading to the parking lot.

"Thanks. I'll let them think they got away, then I'll pounce on them," he said with a wink, then disappeared around the hedge, hot on their trail.

Maggie looked at Dyna, laughed, and shrugged. "Well, I'm off. Again."

"Maggie," Dyna called to her after a moment. When Maggie turned she said, "I just thought I should remind you. Kids and animals almost always are crazy about the town drunk."

Maggie laughed and nodded, but Dyna's face, for once, was serious.

As Maggie climbed into her Dodge Shadow, Dyna's words echoed through her mind. It was true, she admitted, putting the car in gear and backing out of the parking spot. Everyone tends to think you're wonderful if kids like you, but kids—and animals—can't and don't look too deeply.

She pulled onto the white gravel driveway and reached for a sourball from the bag in the console. She drove the twisting roadway, winding her way through the trees, and finally came to the end where the white clapboard sign hung. However, she argued with herself, kids *do* have instincts—often quite good ones.

Maggie unwrapped the cellophane from her candy, then turned onto the mountain road, popping the sourball into her mouth at the same time. Tangy Orange. The road was as empty as it had been the other times she drove it. Maggie took the sharp turns at a leisurely pace, keeping several feet between her car and the guardrail on the right. The sun dappled soft patterns through the trees, and her thoughts soon returned to Rob Clayton. She reran their conversation of the previous night.

She had just come to the part she liked best, their discussion of teaching methods and kids, when something moved in her rearview mirror, and she glanced at it. A large blue van had suddenly appeared on the road behind her. Her eyes went back to the road again as she tried to pick up her thoughts, but in a moment her gaze returned to the mirror. The van had gained on her. Too quickly.

She glanced back and forth several times from the twisting road in front of her to the van reflected in the mirror. It was now close behind her, uncomfortably close. Maggie pressed down on the accelerator and felt herself taking the curves at a speed that made her pulse quicken. Another car shot toward her from around a curve in the opposite lane, edging over the center line, and Maggie jerked her car away from it. The van kept pace.

She tried to see who was driving, but the sun reflected off the dusty windshield, hiding whoever was behind it. "Slow down," she muttered, anger building. *Back off!* Maggie's tires squealed as she rounded a tight curve. She instinctively put her foot on the brake, and as she slowed the van pulled even with her.

She couldn't believe it! Were they crazy, trying to pass her on this twisty road? Maggie imagined a tanker truck coming toward them, just around the bend, and broke into a sweat. Her hands gripped the wheel tightly.

Much of the light was blocked off from her side of the window as the van moved closer to her, looming only inches away. Suddenly Maggie felt a bone-jarring thud. My God, what are they doing?

She grabbed at the wheel as it slipped through her hands. Another sickening thud. The steering wheel spun, and Maggie saw a blur of trees as her car aimed straight for the guardrail and the steep slope beyond.

Chapter Fourteen

The silence was near-perfect, until slowly, tentatively, a single bird began to peep somewhere high in a tree. Maggie's head lay against the steering wheel, unmoving, as the lone bird's chirping was joined by others. Hot sunlight beat through the windshield, and one hand moved up to wipe a drop of sweat trickling toward her eye. She became aware of a lump in her left cheek and touched it with her tongue. Tangy Orange—the sourball she had popped in her mouth just minutes ago. She waited until her heartbeat slowed closer to normal, taking long, deep breaths, listening to the birds, feeling but not thinking, then eased upright and blinked, looking around.

Her car rested tightly against the guardrail, beyond which was the long, steep, wooded slope, the slope she would have plunged down if she hadn't somehow regained control of her steering and speed. It was all a blur of fast action now as she thought back on it, but somehow, miraculously, she had managed through braking, skidding, and frantic steering to avoid a head-on crash into and through the guardrail.

Maggie waited until she felt steady enough, then unbuckled her seatbelt and eased out of the car. There was no sign of the blue van, which didn't surprise her. It had deliberately tried to run her off the road—and down the mountain. She was certain of that. But whoever was driving had decided not to hang around to watch the final results.

Walking to the rear of the car she saw the deep skid marks her tires had made in the gravel. She reached the guardrail and saw some of her car's paint and a series of large dents in it. Then, holding onto the rail to steady her rubbery legs she peered at the side of her car. It was scraped badly and dented, but on the whole, especially considering what might have happened, not too bad. Still, Maggie winced, feeling the pain of an injury to her cherished, yet-unpaid-for car.

Maggie walked around some more, to calm her nerves, her emotions still swinging between anger, amazement, and fear, then back again. When she felt calm enough, she opened the driver's-side door, ready to move on. A tan Plymouth chugged up the road—the only moving thing she had seen since the blue van had loomed up beside her—and she tensed, watching it. It contained an elderly couple, the man in a porkpie hat. They slowed at the sight of her. Then, apparently deciding she needed no help, or perhaps afraid to stop, they continued on.

Maggie turned on the ignition, put the car in gear, and slowly, with nerve-rending scraping noises, pulled onto the road. Listening carefully for any strange knocks or bumps, she gradually relaxed as the engine and wheels responded with no evidence of major damage.

Questions ran through her head as she drove, watching carefully for any sign of the demonic van ahead. Who drove it? Why did they do this? Was it a random act of violence or was it aimed particularly at eliminating her?

And if it were aimed at her, what did they hope to gain by her death?

She thought of how casual—careless, really—she had been with Lori's notebook. So many people had seen it, or perhaps overheard her talking about it with Dyna. Did one of them try to keep her from getting it to the sheriff? She wondered what the sheriff would say about this. Would it move him to more action?

"My, my, my," Sheriff Burger said, clicking his tongue and shaking his head as he read the report Maggie had filled out. He hooked his thumbs into his straining belt and shook his head. "Those roads can be mighty tricky, can't they?"

"Sheriff, I didn't lose control because of the turns. I'm a very good driver. I'd have to be to have avoided plunging down that mountain to my death. I'm telling you someone deliberately tried to force me off the road. I could have been killed!"

"A blue van, you say? Did you happen to get the license number?"

Maggie watched him reach for a pencil, preparing to write, just in case while scrambling to save her life she had managed to glance at, and memorize, the van's tag numbers. She shook her head in exasperation.

"No, I didn't."

"That's too bad." He laid the pencil down in evident disappointment. "A description of the driver?" he asked, with less hope now. Maggie shook her head.

"Well, we'll see what we can do, check up on it."

The phone on his desk rang, and the sheriff picked it up. "Earl, you ol' son-of-a-gun." He listened a moment and laughed a deep, chortling belly laugh. He glanced at Maggie as she waited stiffly, holding Lori's journal on her lap, and turned away slightly. "Let me call you back in a few minutes, Earl," he said, and hung up, swinging back to face Maggie. She put the journal on his desk.

"This belonged to Lori Basker." She explained where it

had been found, avoiding mention of exactly *who* had discovered it, and told of some of the things she had read in it. "I feel strongly that she was murdered by someone who worked with her at the Highview. I also think this same person, or someone closely connected, drove the van that tried to kill me."

"Hmm," the sheriff said, as he pulled the journal to him and paged through it. "Does she say in here that she was afraid of anyone, or maybe threatened by someone?"

"No, there's nothing like that. It's just that, knowing Lori, I think she was probably trying to help someone, and innocently, naively, picked the wrong person. That journal, I think, contains clues to the identity of that person."

"Mm-hmm." The phone rang again, and this time was answered in another part of the office. Before Maggie could say more, though, a deputy called over to announce that the mayor was on the line.

Sheriff Burger put his hand on the phone and looked up at Maggie. "I thank you, ma'am, for bringing this in. And if we find out anything about the blue van we will surely call you. Ah, you'll be at the Highview? You're not going back home soon?"

Maggie shook her head.

"Well, you be careful now, especially on those twisty roads. You be real careful."

His solemn tone surprised her, and she saw a serious look in his eyes. Was it her imagination, or was he now warning her against more than a scraped car?

Maggie nodded automatically, and the sheriff's face quickly crinkled back into a smile. Before she even stood up he was talking cheerfully to the mayor, apparently about arrangements for the Fourth of July parade. Maggie walked to the door, but before going out, she glanced back. Sheriff Burger returned her look and, leaning an elbow on Lori's journal, waved a friendly good-bye.

*   *   *

Maggie drove back to the Highview, checking her mirror often for dark vans, or any vehicle that might seem to be following her. She hated the feeling of paranoia, the jumpy suspicion of any moving thing, that now possessed her, even though she knew it was wise to be careful. As she pulled into the hotel's parking lot, she looked around for any sign of the van and saw none.

Walking quickly from her car to the front door, Maggie checked her watch. It was 11:45. Dyna's aerobics class would have finished long ago. Maggie stopped at the courtesy table in the lobby and poured herself a styrofoam cupful of coffee. Wondering where she might find her friend, she headed down the hall to the exercise room.

There was no sign of Dyna there. One rather paunchy man sat puffing rhythmically at the rowing machine, and a leotard-clad young woman, with a headband securing her hair, stood behind a high desk examining a schedule book. She looked up at Maggie with a shining, freckled face and smiled.

"Can I help you?"

"I'm looking for Dyna Hall. I think she was in the aerobics class."

"Yes, I remember her. Um, she might still be in the jacuzzi." She pointed the way and Maggie went down a short hallway, then opened a door that let out a wave of warm, humid air, causing every curly hair on her head to tighten.

Dyna's head and shoulders protruded from the circulating waters of the jacuzzi, and her eyelids drooped drowsily. Maggie was glad to see her there alone, and pulled a white plastic chair up close. Dyna's eyes focused at the noise and she looked up. "Maggie, you're back!"

"Have a good workout?" Maggie asked, and took a sip of her coffee.

"Terrific. If I did that every day I would be in such good shape. How'd it go at the sheriff's?"

Maggie told her about her near brush with examining the

mountainside treetops close up, and Dyna snapped out of her stupor.

"My gosh, Maggie! You could have been killed!" she said as she straightened up.

Maggie shrugged.

Dyna pulled herself onto the edge of the jacuzzi and searched around for her towel, her silvery-blue suit dripping and catching the light. "You've got to get out of here. I mean, pack up and leave. C'mon, I'll help you, and then I'm coming with you."

Maggie shook her head. "No, Dyna. I'm not ready to leave yet."

Dyna opened her mouth to protest, but Maggie cut her off. "Don't you see? This proves we're getting close. It proves, to me at least, that Lori's murderer is right here. If we run away and do nothing, that person will likely go free. And someone else might be killed."

Dyna pulled her feet up to the jacuzzi edge and hugged her knees, a worried look on her face. "But what if that someone else is you, or me?"

"We'll just have to be careful to avoid that, won't we?" Maggie tried to smile, but her face grew serious again. "I mean, *I'm* going to be careful. Dyna, why don't you go on home after all. I'd feel better if you did."

Dyna stared at her toes for a moment, chin on wet knees, then shook her head and looked up at Maggie. "Uh-uh. I'm not leaving you here alone." She swung her legs to the floor and stood up. "C'mon, let's go back upstairs and I'll get dressed, and we'll figure out our next move."

Back in her room, Maggie noticed the message light blinking on her phone and she called down to the desk. Liz, her librarian friend, had tried to reach her while she was out and left a number. Maggie punched it in and sat down, pulling paper and pen close by, waiting to hear her friend's familiar voice.

"Hi Liz, it's Maggie. You have something for me?"

"Something, Maggie, but not a lot, I'm afraid."

Maggie listened as Liz explained the steps she had taken to find the information, checking newspapers and sports magazines for the time period Maggie had given her.

"He wasn't a big name, so he didn't get that much coverage," she said. What she did find, however, seemed to confirm Eric's claim: Rob Clayton, rising young tennis pro, had abruptly withdrawn from the Wimbledon tournament. No explanation had been given beyond a vague claim of illness, but rumors had floated around about a violent fight with a girlfriend, and police involvement.

"The girl's name was Christy Hammond, a tennis player herself, American, and playing in the Junior's."

"How old was Rob at the time?"

"Um, let's see. Eighteen. Which can be a volatile age for some, as we high school educators know well."

"Mmm. That's it? Nothing about charges actually brought or anything like that?"

"That's it. Again, he wasn't a big name, so the press might not have followed up on it."

"Right. Thanks, Liz. I owe you one." Maggie was about to hang up when she caught herself. "Oh, Liz! How would you feel about looking up a couple more things?"

"Are you kidding? I'd love it! This is the reason I went into library science. It's a great change from the usual junk I have to plow through all summer. You know, counting books, ordering new ones, all that really exciting stuff. Just tell me what you need."

Maggie did.

"Do you want to let me in on what this is all about yet?" Liz asked. "I mean, you didn't take a summer job with the FBI by any chance, did you?"

Maggie laughed. "No, nothing like that. I'm actually on vacation. But you know me, the math perfectionist. If something doesn't add up correctly, it drives me crazy. I'll explain more when I've got a few more numbers, okay?"

"Okay, Maggie. I'll get back to you."

Liz hung up, and Maggie sat next to the phone thinking. Soon she heard a knock on her door and a muffled call through it. "Maggie, it's me."

Maggie let Dyna in, then told her what she had just found out about Rob.

"Doesn't make him sound like a sterling character, does it?" Dyna said.

"No, but it's very incomplete. Mostly rumors and innuendo. Actually, not much more believable than listening to Eric."

"Except, it at least shows he didn't make the *whole* thing up."

"Yes." Maggie scowled at the wall for a moment, then said, "Come on. There's someone I'd like to talk to downstairs."

As they stepped off the elevator in the lobby, Maggie and Dyna saw the silver-haired Charles in his neat navy blazer, checking in a new guest. They sat down on one of the several sofas in the lobby to wait, idly picking up tourist leaflets on a nearby table.

Maggie looked at one that described the Civil War battlefield of Antietam, which was in the area. It looked interesting, and Maggie remembered her hope to visit it during her vacation. "Have you ever been there?" she asked Dyna, holding the brochure up for her to see.

"What is it? History? Ugh, no. I hate those things. Especially anything to do with wars. Upsets my aura."

The business at the desk was apparently completed, as the new arrival picked up one of his smaller bags and followed the rest of his luggage, in the care of a bellboy, to the elevator. Maggie stood up and walked over. Charles glanced up and smiled as he gathered up papers.

"Charles, I was looking for Rob earlier today, about ten, and couldn't find him. Is he off today? I thought maybe I saw him drive away in a dark-colored van."

"No, I'm sure he's here somewhere. And I believe he drives a more *sporty* vehicle—fitting, I suppose," he added with a smile. "A white Miata," Charles said, as he opened an appointment book and scanned it. "Well, he was scheduled for a tennis lesson at ten, with a Mr. Anderson, but, ah yes, now I remember. He called here and asked us to reschedule it for later."

"When did he call, do you remember?" Dyna had come up beside her by now.

"Yes, it was shortly before ten. I remember because we nearly didn't reach Mr. Anderson in time to tell him. It's rather unusual for Rob to do something like that. He's quite conscientious. So something rather important must have come up at the last minute."

"Yes," Maggie murmured. "I'm sure it must have been something important."

She avoided looking at Dyna's eyes.

Chapter Fifteen

"You're fighting it, Maggie."

"Dyna, I really think I'm just trying to keep an open mind." They were having a quick lunch in the dining room and discussing their recent findings quietly. Guests filled most of the tables around them—apparently everyone had hunger pains at the same time.

Dyna took a huge bite from her pita bread sandwich and chewed for a while. "You know, Rob *was* around when you were telling me about Lori's journal this morning at breakfast. He could have overheard us from the other side of the the hedge. Or maybe one of the kids said something about it. Remember, the first boy knocked it out of your hands, then picked it up?"

She looked thoughtful for a moment. "No, scratch that. They wouldn't have cared about some old journal. So Rob probably overheard it all. Then, he cancels his lesson, hops in the van, and tries to force you and your car down the mountainside before you can take the journal to the sheriff."

"But where did he get a van? Charles said he drives a Miata."

"Minor point. We'll figure that one out later. Maybe he borrowed it from a friend."

"Oh, I see. As in, 'Pardon me, would you mind if I used your van for a few minutes? I need to run someone off the road right now.' "

Dyna grinned. "That's a very defensive joke, Maggie. I think you agree with me, but you don't like it."

"You may have some good points, Dyna. But that doesn't mean you're one hundred percent right. And just as in math, *almost* right just doesn't cut it with murder cases. I just need more facts before I start making conclusions. I'd like to try to find that van. Want to help me look?"

"Where? Around here?"

"Yes. At least to start. Maybe it came from somewhere else, but it obviously was very accessible to whoever decided to take off after me."

"Yeah, after he shook off the two kids."

"Dyna, please keep an open mind." Maggie pushed back her chair.

"I will as long as you do, too." Dyna followed Maggie from the dining room. "Remember, if he killed Lori, he won her trust first. Made her think he was this super-nice guy who just needed the help of a good woman."

Maggie had to admit that that could be true. *If* he killed Lori. She was still keeping a big *if* in her mind.

They walked around the outside of the hotel, checking first the back parking lot, then the side, and found only the usual midsize cars and a station wagon or two. One thin, gray-haired woman, who had just driven in and parked, climbed out of her Volvo and looked over at them curiously.

"Did you lose something, dears?" she called, her face puckered in kindly concern.

"Just trying to remember where I parked," Maggie assured her.

"Oh, I do that all the time." She smiled at them with understanding, pushed the strap of her bulging purse over her forearm, and walked toward the hotel.

Maggie saw Dyna looking at her and shrugged. "What was I going to say? That we're searching for a large vehicle with a murderer at the wheel?"

"No, I guess not." Dyna grinned. "Not unless you're good at CPR, anyway. She would have fainted on the spot. Let's go check the front."

They left that parking lot and circled to the front, shoes crunching on the gravel. There was less shade here, and the temperature jumped about ten degrees. Maggie looked over the lot, her eyes squinting at the glare. No blue van in sight. An empty luggage cart banged out the front door, pushed by one of the bellboys, and Maggie hurried over, heading him off.

"Have you seen a dark blue van parked here in the last day or so?" she asked.

"Dark blue? No, the only van around here is that one over there." He pointed to a cream-colored van at the end of the row which was spewing out its contents of bags, tennis racquets, beach balls, and children.

"I thought I saw a blue one leaving here this morning. Does anyone who works here have one?"

"Well, maintenance has vans. I think some of them are blue. Maybe you saw one of them."

"Maintenance? Where are they kept?" Maggie asked nonchalantly, covering the intensity of her interest.

"Over there, next to those buildings out there." He pointed to an area west of the hotel, and Maggie put her hand to her eyes to shade them and looked over a large expanse of lawn that she had never crossed. She saw outbuildings in the distance.

"Thanks," she said. The young man shrugged, smiled shyly, and continued on his way to help the family with the cream-colored van unload. Maggie looked over at Dyna, whose face reflected her own excitement, and they took off over the grass.

As they walked toward the isolated buildings, Maggie realized how glad she was that Dyna had stayed to help with her investigation. She was aware of how dangerous this could be for her to come here alone, unarmed. Unarmed! The thought of needing a weapon made her shiver. She rubbed at goose bumps on her arms at the same time that a trickle of sweat formed at her brow from the hot sun beating down on her.

They approached the two buildings and saw a gravel road leading to the other side of the closest one, possibly connecting with the road that led out to the highway. Large overhead doors stood open on the side they could see, exposing lawn equipment, work tables, and tools. No one appeared to be inside.

Maggie and Dyna peeked in, picking up pungent odors of gasoline and oil. But seeing nothing of interest there, they left and walked around to where the gravel road led. There, side by side, baking in the sun, were two dark blue vans.

"Ohmigosh! Is that it?"

"One of them is. As far as I can tell, anyway." Maggie supressed a shudder as she looked at them, the memory of that dark shape looming up close to her own car rushing back to her. She took a deep breath, then went to examine the vans closely. There were scrapes and dents on both, but it was impossible to tell when they might have been acquired. She saw none of her car's dark red paint on either van, but she noticed that one had been very recently washed. The windows of both were rolled down, and keys hung from their ignitions.

"These are both ripe for picking." Maggie ran a hand through her hair in exasperation. "Anyone could walk over here and just take off with either one." She glanced around and saw a door in the second building that looked like it led to an office. "Maybe somebody's there who can tell us something," she said, and led the way over to it.

The office was small, cluttered, and unoccupied. "Hello," Dyna called out as they walked in. No one responded.

"Here's something." On the wall near the door Maggie found a sign-out sheet for the vans. One had been taken out at eight-fifteen that morning and returned at nine-thirty by a Merle Walker. After that the sheet was blank.

"Just our luck. Our murderer didn't sign out his vehicle properly," Maggie said with a rueful smile.

"Don't you just hate it when they don't follow the rules?" Dyna said.

"What are you doing in there?" A loud voice barked at them from outside. Dyna jumped, and Maggie swung around. She saw a tall, sinewy man charging towards the door and recognized Jack, the gardener she had spoken to about Eric. He didn't have a patient smile on his face this time, but a challenging, angry scowl. Maggie lifted her chin. In ordinary circumstances she would have no right to be poking around here. But these were no ordinary circumstances.

"What are you doing in here?" he repeated as he stopped in the doorway.

"We were looking for a blue van, which we found, out there."

"A van? What for?"

"I had a very close call this morning, driving down to Coopersburg. A blue van tried to push me off the road. I wanted to find it, and its driver."

The anger on Jack's face disappeared, his eyes suddenly

showing worry and something else. Maggie wasn't sure just
what. "You think it was one of our vans?"

"It's possible. I can't tell for sure. Do you know if anyone took one out about ten this morning?"

"I don't know. I was busy putting in some new azaleas
over on the other side of the hotel. What about . . ." He
reached for the sign-out sheet.

"There's nothing filled in for that time. Whoever took it
didn't leave tracks."

Jack put both hands on his face and rubbed at his eyes.
He looked very unhappy. "Bob Hill's supposed to be here,
watching things, but he's out sick today." He squinted in
the direction of the gravel road. "You really think it was
one of our vans?"

"Well, how many dark blue vans are there in this little
corner of the world? We didn't see any parked in the guest
parking lots. And it was behind me very soon after I had
left the hotel."

"Did you report this to anyone?"

"Yes. The sheriff. He said he'll look into it."

"Good. I'd talk to Ms. Crawford about it, too. She was
gone for a meeting this morning, but she might be back by
now. She should know about this." Jack's expression said
that ended the discussion, and he started to turn away.

"Wait. Could we talk a bit?"

"What?" Impatience was in his voice now. "I already
told you I was busy somewhere else this morning."

"I'm wondering about Eric Semple. Remember, we
talked about him before?"

"Eric? What about him?"

"Do you know where he was about that time?"

Jack scratched his head. His mouth had turned down
about as far as it could go. Maggie got the distinct impression he didn't want to talk about Eric, and that he was
aching to get away from her. "I can't say for sure. I sent
him over to work on some hedges, but I don't follow my

helpers around to make sure they're doing everything I tell them to do."

"Was he out of your sight between ten and eleven?"

"I don't know. Maybe. Who watches the time? Look, I gotta go. I'm sorry about your accident, Miss. Maybe the sheriff will track it all down."

Jack left them and walked into the tool storage area. They heard puttering noises, then the sound of a motor starting. Jack came chugging out on a riding mower, wearing ear protectors and a grim expression. He looked determinedly straight ahead, away from them.

"Eric?" Dyna asked as they watched him go. "You think Eric might have been the one?"

"It's just a guess. We'll have to find out more. But did you notice Jack didn't leap to Eric's defense?"

Maggie gazed after the receding mower. "I think he might have his suspicions too."

Maggie and Dyna turned back to the hotel, walking in silence for a while.

"At least we know for sure now that someone here at the Highview is involved," Dyna said. "Rob could have run over and jumped in one of the vans by the time you were pulling out of the parking lot. That gravel road probably put him right in back of you on the hotel driveway."

"But Eric works in maintenance, don't forget. He would be more aware of the availability of the vans."

"But why would Eric want to hurt you?"

Maggie shook her head but didn't say anything. Something had caught her eye over to the side. She turned to see a figure some distance away walking rapidly toward the hotel. It seemed to Maggie from the angle of his route that he came from the maintenance buildings they had just left.

"Hello," she called. The figure didn't stop or turn around, but instead picked up his pace.

They watched for a moment, then Maggie said, "Isn't that our waiter from this morning? Remember, Chuck?"

Dyna squinted. "Yeah, I think you're right. What would he be doing here?"

"That's what I'm wondering too."

Too many questions. Too few answers. Maggie sighed. The analytical part of her brain had become weary. Looking ahead she caught sight of the hotel's pool in the distance, its blue water glinting invitingly in the sun, and she realized how hot and tired she felt.

"How about taking some time off from our investigation and having a swim?"

Dyna's eyes lit up in agreement, and they picked up their pace to get back to their rooms and change to their suits. Soon they were plunging into the cool water. Maggie swam laps while Dyna floated lazily on her back, soaking up the warmth of the sun on her face.

Maggie found the vigorous excercise relaxing, releasing pent-up tension she had barely been aware of, so intent had she been on the recent happenings. She swam for several minutes until she was out of breath, then pulled herself out of the pool and collapsed on a lounge chair.

The exhaustion felt good, and she didn't want to think about murder and murderers for now. She didn't want to think about her brother, Joe, worrying about her, or feel guilty at the thought of her mother, who still didn't know what Maggie was involved in. She just wanted to rest and let her mind go blank. She needed to gaze at the sky or the water, breathe in the flower-scented air, and pretend all was right with the world. For now.

Chapter Sixteen

That evening, relaxed and refreshed, Maggie and Dyna were finishing a late dinner in the dining room. Only a few other tables were occupied, and the atmosphere was unrushed. Dyna, wearing a short denim jumper and T-shirt tonight, pushed away a plate with the few remaining crumbs of her dessert, a rich cherry pie, and groaned. "That just undid all my efforts in aerobics class this morning." She grinned. "But it was worth it."

"Why don't you take the class again tomorrow morning? I'm going to drive down to Lori's funeral."

"Oh." Dyna looked at Maggie with troubled eyes. "I know why you want to, but do you think it's a good idea? I mean, driving down that road again?"

"I know, I've thought of that. But I talked to a couple at the pool this afternoon, the McManuses. They're planning to check out and leave just about the time I need to go. I asked them if I could follow them to the turnoff to Coopersburg. I didn't want to upset them with the whole story, so I made an excuse about having a terrible sense of direction."

"Good idea." Dyna's face took on a faraway look. "Actually, you know, *I* have an awful sense of direction. I'm always getting lost." She picked up her fork to lick the last few crumbs from it. "The worst time was when I drove home one night from New Jersey where some friends had moved. They had a, you know, housewarming. Anyway, it was late and I remember I was tired and I kept turning up the radio to keep awake. So, I came down I-95 and I guess I missed a few signs 'cause I thought I was on the Baltimore beltway, but somehow I had gone all the way down to the Washington beltway. There I was, driving around and around for half the night looking for my exit until I finally figured out where I was."

Maggie tried not to laugh out loud at her friend, but she couldn't hold back a grin. "Well, they both go in circles, don't they?"

"Exactly! I must have crossed the Wilson Bridge three times before I realized it wasn't the Key Bridge. I kept wondering what had happened to the toll booths."

They had left the dining room and were strolling down the hallway. Sounds of country music drifted out of the lounge—livelier now than it had been two nights ago—and Maggie glanced in as they came to it. She saw Rob seated at the bar alone.

They passed the doorway and Dyna's tale had moved on to the problems she had finding airports, and particularly the people she had gone to pick up. "My mom said she'd wait at the curb so I wouldn't have to park, and it was windy and raining, and here I was—"

"Rob's back there," Maggie interrupted, "in the bar. This might be a good chance to talk to him." She stopped, thinking for a moment. "I think I'd like to do it alone. Do you mind?"

"No-o," Dyna said, throwing a nervous glance toward the doorway. "But how about I stay close by?"

"There's no need," Maggie assured her. "There are plenty of other people in the lounge."

Dyna looked unconvinced. "I could be out here, just walking around. I don't mind."

"No, Dyna, really. I'll be perfectly fine."

"Promise to stay there and not be lured into a midnight stroll or something?"

"Promise. Cross my heart and . . . well, anyway, I promise."

"Okay then. But call me as soon as you get back to your room, will you?"

Maggie nodded and waited as Dyna turned back to the lobby, looking back once with an I-wish-you-weren't-doing-this look on her face. Maggie grinned, then took a deep breath and walked into the lounge. There was an empty stool next to Rob, and she slid onto it.

"Hi."

Rob looked over in surprise, and a smile instantly appeared on his face. He wore shorts and a polo shirt, and his sockless feet were in well-worn boat shoes. She noticed that his eyes looked tired, and a little sad. She didn't see any signs of guilt or uneasiness at seeing her, though. Either he *wasn't* the driver in that van, or he was amazingly cool about it.

"I saw you sitting here and thought I'd say hello."

"Glad you did. Can I get you something?"

"No, thanks. I just finished dinner." The bartender, Dave, looked over in her direction, but she shook her head. "There's something I'd like to talk to you about. Could we move over to one of the tables where it's quieter?"

"Sure," he said, looking at her curiously. He picked up his glass and followed her over to a table some distance from the jukebox and from other seated customers. "What's up?" he asked as soon as they settled down.

"Well," Maggie leaned her arms on the table wondering how to begin. "You'll probably think this is none of my business, and you can tell me to butt out and I'll completely understand. However, Eric Semple made some pretty nasty allegations about you the other day, and I just wondered if you'd like to clear them up."

Rob's face darkened, and his lips pressed together. "Eric! What the hell's he been going around saying about me?" He said it with anger, but controlled anger, and Maggie felt encouraged to go on.

"Remember you told me about playing at Wimbledon? You never said exactly why you had to bow out. Eric implied that you had been in trouble with the police. Something about a girlfriend, and a fight which became violent, and her bringing charges." Maggie held her breath, waiting to see how Rob would react, what he would say. She realized she hoped he would explain it all, that there would be nothing at all to it.

Rob's face hardened, and he looked up at the ceiling, then back at her. What he finally said blotted out all the other sounds of the lounge, as though a heavy, dark curtain had dropped around her. "How did he find out about that?"

"You mean it's true?" Maggie's voice had lowered almost to a whisper. From the jukebox Reba McIntyre finished her song, and guitars twanged a final chord.

"Some of it." Rob looked steadily into Maggie's eyes. He took a deep breath. "There was a fight, but only a verbal one. I did not hit her, as she claimed. There was trouble with the police because she tried to stir some up. She was a good-looking, spoiled brat of a sixteen-year-old, a good tennis player, and my coach's daughter."

"Your coach's daughter," Maggie repeated, starting to understand.

"Right. Bad judgment on my part, but I was eighteen, and pretty full of myself at the time. Maybe I was as much of a brat as she was, I don't know. But I do know we both had short fuses." Rob took a drink from his glass and gazed at it for a moment. Then he looked back up at Maggie.

"There were plenty of arguments between us, but I never hit her. The final one happened when I caught her smoking pot. I never could stand the thought of drugs. Even back then I knew that getting into drugs was throwing your life down the tubes. So when I caught her using, I blew up.

"I tried to scare her, threatened to tell her father, whatever it took to get her to quit. She didn't like that—couldn't stand someone trying to control her, I guess—so she fought back, hard. After I left her, she made it look like she'd been beat up, showed up with bruises on her arms, a cut on her face, a fat lip. Don't ask me how she did it—she must have been desperate and a little crazy. Anyway, her father—my coach—hit the roof and called the police. He wouldn't listen to anything I had to say. His daughter was his perfect princess."

A man and woman stood up at their table nearby and Rob waited until they had walked by.

"There was bad publicity, and the tournament officials got in on the act. Suggested to me, oh so politely, that it would be better for me to withdraw." Rob let out a bitter laugh. "I think they meant better for them."

He took a long swallow from his glass, and Maggie now wished she had ordered something to drink. Her mouth had become very dry. Rob's story struck her as very believable. Or did she just *want* to believe it?

"Things just kind of spiraled downward from then on," Rob continued. "My coach had a lot of pull. It's amazing how many people believe half-truths and anything in print. And I guess I couldn't handle it either. Just gave up after a while. And that was the end of my pro playing career."

"What happened to your girlfriend?"

Rob took another drink from his glass and let out a heavy sigh. "She played a couple more years. Then I heard she checked into a rehab place somewhere. Guess her father finally figured it out. Too late for me, though."

Maggie looked across at Rob. "I'm sorry."

Rob looked back a moment, then reached his hand out to cover hers and smiled. "Thanks. You're probably the first person to listen to my side of the story with an open mind."

Maggie smiled, and enjoyed the touch of his hand on hers. His hand was large and covered hers easily, which made her feel warm and good. She slowly pulled hers away, however, reminding herself of one more thing she needed to ask him.

"I don't want to get Eric in trouble with you, if you don't mind. I mean, please don't fire him because of what I told you."

Rob scowled, but nodded. "He's a total jerk, but I always knew that. He'll probably take himself off to greener pastures sooner or later anyway, saving me the trouble."

Maggie leaned back in her chair and smiled, planning to change the subject and wanting to sound as though she were simply lightening up the conversation, making social chit-chat. But it was much more than that to her. What Rob said next could make all the difference. "By the way, after we bumped into each other on the patio this morning— when you were chasing after the twins?—Dyna said the hotel people were looking around for a Mr. Anderson. Something about a ten o'clock lesson with you. They seemed to have trouble locating him. Did he finally show up?" Charles's words of how Rob had canceled that lesson at the last minute, just before she left for her near-fatal ride to the sheriff's, played through Maggie's head as she waited for his answer.

"Anderson?" Rob asked. "Oh, yeah. No problem. Guy needs a lot of work on his forehand."

Chapter Seventeen

Maggie slowly followed the McManuses' blue Mercedes down the same twisty mountain road of the day before. She was paying the price now for having overplayed the excuse of a directional disability. Before they left, Mr. McManus had explained to her repeatedly how he would slow down and signal at the point where she should turn off for Coopersburg. And he seemed to fear that she would somehow lose him if he drove at a normal speed.

Maggie tapped her nails on the steering wheel with impatience at his slow, careful pace, willing him to pick things up. But then they came to the spot with the dented guardrail and skid marks. It graphically reminded her of the reason she was going through all this, and she looked on Mr. McManus's presence with a properly grateful eye.

True to his word, McManus slowed even more at the turnoff spot, put on his blinker, beeped his horn, and pointed, along with his wife, to the right. In addition to all this, Maggie saw the same clear road sign that had always been there, directing her to Coopersburg. She grinned, waved a thank-you, and beeped back, watching them continue on with concerned backward glances as she turned.

Maggie drove on alone, at first aware of a slight uneasiness at the loss of her unwitting bodyguards, but gradually relaxing as traffic increased and houses and businesses appeared. As she drove, her thoughts went back to last night's talk with Rob, and they weren't happy thoughts.

Why had he lied? He definitely implied that the lesson with Mr. Anderson had taken place as scheduled. And Maggie knew it had not. Her sympathies had all been with him until then, as he told his side of the Wimbledon story. She was so sure he was being truthful about that. And then he lied. Did that mean he had lied about it all?

She drove farther into town and decided to put those distressing thoughts on hold for a while as she realized she must be getting close to the church. Maggie mentally reviewed the directions Lori's Aunt Rose had given her over the phone. As she drove down Main Street she recognized Green Street, where the Baskers lived, passed it, and continued on about a half-mile. After that she didn't need any more help, as the sight of a gathering crowd of dark-clothed mourners told her that she had found it. Maggie parked and joined the crowd slowly filing into the church.

The service was emotional and moving, as any funeral for one so young would be. The mourners included people of all ages, but those who seemed most affected, aside from Lori's parents, were in Lori's own age group. Maggie recognized more than one young worker from the Highview, particularly Holly, who was wearing a dark green dress and a very somber expression. Maggie also was surprised to see the new waiter, Chuck. If he had been hired after Lori's death, he wouldn't have known her, would he? She looked at him, thinking that lately he seemed to show up in very unexpected places. She also checked carefully, more than once, but did not see Rob among the mourners.

Near the end, a young man played the tape of a popular song, announcing it to have been Lori's favorite. Maggie didn't recognize it, but it seemed to affect Lori's friends greatly as she heard muffled sobs and saw tissues dabbed at eyes. Maggie was taking deep breaths by this time, trying hard to keep her composure. But images of Lori sitting in class, first row, third desk, working out a geometry problem and never knowing how short her life would be, made it difficult.

Finally the casket was wheeled down the church aisle, followed tearfully by family and friends, and the funeral cortege slowly lined up and left for the cemetery.

After the graveside ceremony ended, Maggie waited her turn to speak to Lori's parents.

Mrs. Basker took her hand. "I'm so sorry," was all Maggie could say. It sounded hollow and useless to her, but Lori's mother seemed to receive it gratefully. Her eyes were dry and sunken, as if all emotion had already been wrung out of her, but she reached out and hugged Maggie, who gulped and fought back the moistness springing to her own eyes.

Mr. Basker simply shook her hand and nodded, saying, "Thank you, thank you," and Maggie moved away, feeling at this point unworthy of his gratitude. She hoped she would be able to change that.

She stood aside, waiting until the crowd thinned, and gazed at the mounds of colorful flowers that had accumulated. As she waited, it occurred to her how uplifting these bright bouquets were to the pervading sorrow, and she wondered why dark clothes instead of bright-colored ones became the norm for funerals. She herself had chosen the most subdued skirt and blouse she had packed, white and navy blue. Perhaps I'll put in my will that everyone who comes to my funeral must dress in bright reds and yellows, she thought. Would they? she wondered. She shook off the odd thought as she finally saw Aunt Rose, standing alone. Maggie went up to her.

"Oh, Miss," Rose said, brightening despite reddened eyes. "We're having some food back at the house. Would you like to come over?"

Maggie thought about the large crowd that likely would be there. Her presence wouldn't be needed or missed, and she felt pretty wrung out emotionally. "Thank you, no."

Rose nodded, understanding. "This surely isn't what you had in mind for a vacation, is it?"

Maggie shook her head and smiled. "Have the Baskers heard anything from the sheriff—about the investigation?" she asked.

"Hardly anything. I got John, my husband, to call, but all he found out is that they're working on it." Rose sighed and wiped her pink, glistening face with a handkerchief pulled out of her sleeve.

"I've been asking questions myself," Maggie said, "up at the hotel, trying to fit a few pieces together about what led to Lori's death. Do you know anything about the tennis instructor, Rob Clayton?"

"Rob Clayton," Rose repeated, thinking. "I do remember Lori talking some about him. Let's see, a nice-looking fellow. I think she liked him all right."

"Did she know him well? Perhaps date him?"

"Now that I couldn't tell you for sure. Let me think. She did have a certain sparkle in her eye when she talked about him, but I can't say she ever actually went out with him. Her mother would know, I'm sure. Would you like me to ask her?"

"Yes, when it's a good time. What about Eric Semple? Did Lori ever mention him?"

"Eric Semple? The boy who works in maintenance?"

"Yes, that's him."

"I remember meeting the mother at the blood drive Lori helped organize. The boy I didn't meet, but she pointed him out to me. My, you'd think he had walked on water to get there by the way his mother talked about him. I've known some proud mothers in my time, but usually they had more to work with."

"You weren't too impressed with Eric?"

"Not by looking at him, that's for sure. He has a kind of slouchy, smirky way about him, you know? And Lori couldn't tell me much of anything positive when I asked her later, although she tried. I could see she really tried. Lori liked to see the best in people."

Maggie caught sight of a familiar figure moving in the distance. "Rose, that fellow over there, near the angel monument. He recently started working at the Highview and I didn't think he would know Lori. Does he look familiar?"

Rose turned to see. "Chuckie Henderson? Oh, sure he knew Lori. He had a real crush on her back in high school. I remember she used to complain about his coming around so much, 'cause she really wasn't interested in him, not in that way."

Maggie looked after the retreating Chuckie with greater interest. "How did he take her rejection?"

"Oh, all right, I guess. He eventually stopped calling, but I don't think he ever really gave up hope. Poor boy."

Rose glanced back at the departing family cars. "I'd better get moving now. You try to enjoy the rest of your vacation, now. Just move on from all this, hear?"

Maggie nodded and watched her go, then went in search of her own car. So Chuckie Henderson had a thing for Lori. An obsession, she wondered? Something else to look into. Maggie sat thinking in her car, her hands on the steering wheel, waiting for a chance to pull onto the cemetery road filled now with other departing cars, when she heard her name called. Looking around, she saw Holly scurrying with some difficulty in her high heels on the grass, waving her purse to catch Maggie's attention. She came to the curb, stepped down carefully, and hobbled over to Maggie's open window.

"Can I hitch a ride with you?" she asked, as she bent down and squinted at Maggie. She paused to catch her breath and looked, Maggie thought, like a little girl playing dress-up, with her wide eyes and the few freckles dotted over her nose. "The guy I came with wants to go over to Hagerstown. We both got the afternoon off, but I don't feel like following him around while he shops for car parts. Could you just drop me at my mom's house? It's not much out of the way, honest."

"Sure," Maggie said, and leaned over to unlock the passenger door. Holly stood up and waved an "okay" signal to someone in the distance, then scrambled around and into the car. She started to pull out a cigarette, but Maggie shook her head and pointed to the "No Smoking" sign she had installed the first day she brought her new car home. There weren't a lot of things she was fussy about, but keeping the lingering smell of stale smoke out of her car was one of them. "I don't mind waiting if you want to smoke it outside, though," she said.

"Nah, I should cut down anyway." Holly pushed the cigarettes back into her purse, then leaned back, slipped off her shoes, and gazed out the window as Maggie slowly wound her way out of the cemetery, following a long line of cars. "You can take a right, then a left at that light there," she directed as they finally drove through the gate, then turned to Maggie with a sudden idea. "Hey, you feel like stopping for something to eat first? I'm dying for a cheeseburger. My mom's not expecting me, and there's probably gonna be nothing in the fridge."

"Sounds good to me." Suddenly the thought of greasy fast food made Maggie hungry. "Where's a good place?"

Holly directed Maggie on a zigzag route through the town to a small lunchroom situated snugly between a hardware store and a dress shop. It seemed to be a favorite of

Coopersburg workers and homebodies alike. As they walked in, Maggie saw men in overalls, mothers with small children, and white-haired women in hand-crocheted sweaters sitting at various tables. Red-checked curtains framed the windows, and pictures of the owners' family and pets decorated the walls. Maggie and Holly seated themselves at a table next to the window, and Maggie pulled up the well-thumbed menu propped between the sugar dispenser and salt and pepper shakers. She decided on a chicken salad while Holly stuck with a cheeseburger, and they gave their orders to the young waitress who scurried over with glasses of water and utensils. They made small talk as they waited, turning inevitably to the funeral.

"That really got me at the end, that song, 'Summer Rain,' " Holly said at one point. "I was fine until then. I remembered her humming it as she loaded her trays." Holly's eyes welled up at the memory and she looked away and out the window. Their food came just then, and as plates were set down, Maggie searched for a change of subject.

"Lori's Aunt Rose and I talked for a while at the cemetery, and it turns out she had met Burnelle. It sounds like Burnelle is pretty wrapped up in her son Eric."

Holly snorted. "You could say that. I'd say Burnelle thinks the sun rises and falls according to what Eric is doing each day." She took a bite of her cheeseburger and chewed on it. "She got him his job, you know, and the way she talks you'd think he was head landscaper instead of assistant groundsperson."

Holly slurped at her shake, then looked up at Maggie, grinning at a memory. "Once he got chewed out for something, I don't know what—maybe he dug up the wrong plants or something. Well, he complained to Mama, and she goes running to the manager saying Eric's boss was obviously incompetent, that he couldn't give clear instructions, and so on. Well, I hear the supervisor got a warning, and Eric's been digging up whatever he pleased since then."

Maggie winced. She had come across a few mothers like that at school. They thought they were doing the right thing for their kids, getting them out of detentions, blaming their failures on their teachers. Instead of helping, however, the kids often ended up with even more problems in their life.

"Was that supervisor Jack?" she asked.

Holly looked up, surprised. "Yeah. You know Jack?"

Maggie nodded. She knew Jack didn't like Eric much, and was uneasy talking about him. This was one good reason, but Maggie had the feeling there was even more to it.

"What do you think of Eric?" Maggie asked.

"Me? I barely know him. I try to keep my distance from both of them, him and his mother." Holly started digging in her purse for her cigarettes, and Maggie sensed she was being evasive.

"Holly, you know I'm trying to find out as much about the hotel and the people there as I can because I want to identify Lori's murderer. I've had some questions about Eric but haven't found out very much about him yet. Anything you could add might make a big difference."

"Yeah, well, I wish I could help you, but I can't." Holly took a long drag on her cigarette and looked away with a stony expression that said the subject was closed. Maggie was puzzled, but decided to drop it, at least for now. She finished her lunch, nibbling at the remaining potato chips and dill pickle, keeping the conversation light and neutral. Holly gradually loosened up again, and by the time they were back in the car she was chattering cheerfully.

She started giving Maggie directions to her mother's house when she stopped. "You know what?" she said. "If I go there, there's probably going to be nobody home, or if there is, my mom and me will find something to get in a fight about. I'd rather do something different, go somewhere. What do you think?"

Maggie looked over, surprised. "You mean with me?"

"Yeah, if you want. You got to get back to the hotel for something?"

"No," Maggie considered. "I guess not. Not right away, anyway. What did you have in mind?"

"I don't know. It's your car. You decide. Anything, as long as it's not Hagerstown, shopping for tires."

"Hagerstown. Doesn't Rob's mother live there?"

"Yeah, I think he mentioned that once. But I don't think he grew up there 'cause he didn't seem to know the town too well. So, where should we go?"

Maggie thought for a minute, then grinned at Holly. "I don't know about you but I know what I'd like to do. It's something I thought about when I was first driving up here. I'd like to go see Antietam."

"Antietam? The battlefield?"

"Yes. Have you ever been there?"

"Oh, yeah. They dragged us there once in junior high. I don't remember much about it, just a lot of cornfields and stuff."

"Do you mind going again? I've never been."

Holly thought a moment, then kicked off her shoes. "Sure, why not? Maybe there'll be a couple of cute guys there, who knows."

Maggie laughed and handed the map to her. "Get me there in twenty minutes and they're both yours."

As they drove, Maggie hoped spending this time with Holly, talking about unrelated things, would gradually win over the girl's trust and she would divulge things that Maggie was sure she was holding back. She had had success with that method once or twice at school, talking to a student who seemed unmotivated about schoolwork, gradually finding out, through casual after-class chats about practically nothing, what the real problem was. Maggie's final goal this time, though, was much greater than raising grades.

They pulled into the parking lot of the visitors' center in exactly seventeen minutes and Maggie joked about the right incentives producing great results. "Looks like the cute guys haven't got here yet, though," she said, glancing at the scattered tourists, "unless those two will do?" She pointed out a pair of toddlers in sailor suits, riding in the stroller pushed by their mother, and Holly laughed.

Maggie spotted the pay phone in front of the center and, climbing out of the car, said, "Just give me a minute." She thought she'd better call Dyna and let her know about her detour so she wouldn't worry. Dyna was getting more and more mother-hen-like, which Maggie found both comforting and amusing.

She fished change from her skirt pocket, pushed the coins into the slot, and dialed the Highview. Maggie had a quirky but handy memory for phone numbers, part of her natural bent for numbers in general, she figured. "Normal people remember names and faces, Maggie remembers birthdates and phone numbers," Joe often teased. Having called the Highview once for her reservations, the number was now etched in her mind. She asked the hotel operator to connect her with Dyna's room, and when, not surprisingly, there was no answer, she left a message saying she'd be back late in the afternoon.

She and Holly strolled into the visitors' center, looked around at the memorabilia for a while, then rented a tape player and cassette for a driving tour of the area.

They drove off from the center slowly, following the sign to the first designated stop, Dunker Church. It sat peacefully near the road surrounded by a tidy green lawn, with a cannon sitting nearby the only testament that something other than prayer and church picnics had taken place there at one time. They listened to the voice on the cassette recount the skirmishes that had occurred there, then drove slowly on, following arrows on the road to the next stop.

Maggie noticed Holly's expression changing gradually

from polite boredom to interested involvement as the tour progressed.

"Why'd they just march up to each other like that? They were getting shot like crazy," she said at one point, after hearing about the battle in the Miller cornfield, where, in the words of General Hooker, ". . . the slain lay in rows precisely as they had stood in their ranks a few moments before."

"I read somewhere that they still followed outmoded battle tactics that had been used for centuries when men fought with swords or bare hands."

"Well, jeez! You'd think when they saw half their armies done in in the first few minutes they'd think, hey, maybe we should try something different."

"I agree."

They drove past the Mumma farm, some of whose buildings had been burned during the battle, and to the sunken road, also called Bloody Lane because of the large number of casualties—five thousand—that had resulted there.

"My gosh, I never knew that!" Holly said, astonished. "How come they never told us that when I was here?"

"Maybe they did, but you were busy batting your eyes at some twelve-year-old Leonardo DiCaprio," Maggie teased.

Holly grinned. "Yeah, I probably was. How'd you know that?"

Maggie's eyes crinkled. "Just a guess."

They went to the remaining stops, ending with the Antietam National Cemetery. Holly gazed with round eyes at the endless rows of white crosses. "Gosh. All that from one battle?"

Maggie nodded. "And these are only the Union soldiers buried here. And not all of them, either. Some, I suppose, were returned to their families."

Holly looked at the rows upon rows of graves, shading her eyes with her hand. She spun around suddenly and started walking back to the car. "C'mon, let's go, huh? This is depressing."

They returned the tape player to the visitors' center, then got back in the car. Maggie checked the map, then glanced at her watch as Holly looked quietly out her window.

"We still have some time, I think, before you have to get back. I've noticed that the John Brown farmhouse is not far from here. There're no graves there, I promise. Like to see it?"

Holly looked over, shrugged, and smiled. "Sure, why not." As they drove, she said to Maggie, "You know, there's so much I don't know, and it's stupid because I should. You were right about me probably fooling around instead of paying attention. That's how I went through all those years—just not paying attention. You know, I never finished high school."

"No, I didn't know. That's too bad."

"Yeah, well, it seemed like a good idea at the time, to drop out. I mean, my grades were the pits, and it all just seemed a waste of time. I sometimes wish, though, that I could go back and do it all over."

Maggie had loads of teacherly advice she could have offered, but she sensed that Holly wasn't looking for advice just then. She had the feeling Holly had to figure a few things out for herself. She was about to make a neutral comment when Holly abruptly changed the subject.

"By the way, remember I told you I'd ask around about Rob? See if he had any connection with that girl who died from an overdose at the hotel?"

Maggie's mind quickly switched gears to keep up with Holly, and she remembered their conversation when Holly brought her Lori's journal. She nodded.

"Well, nobody seemed to remember anything between them. And if you want my personal opinion, you're on the wrong track if you think Rob had anything to do with Lori's murder."

"Oh? Why do you say that?"

"It's just he's an okay guy. There's no way he could do anything like that."

Maggie glanced over at Holly, who met her eyes with wide open ones of her own. "An okay guy? I remember you describing Eric Semple that way when I first asked you about him. Now you seem to have a different opinion. You said during lunch that you try to keep your distance from him. Did something happen in the last two days? Any problem, I mean, with Eric?"

"No," Holly answered shortly, looking away, and Maggie felt the curtain come down again. She decided not to push it.

The John Brown farmhouse was a simple frame, clapboard house. Brown had rented it the summer of 1859, just before his famous raid on Harper's Ferry, a friendly, white-haired female guide told Maggie and Holly as they strolled through the old rooms.

"It was here Brown and his followers, including two of his sons, planned their raid on the U.S. Arsenal, a raid conducted with thirteen white and five black men."

Brown, she said, had had a lifelong opposition to slavery. His own father had tried to forcibly free slaves in Connecticut in 1798. Some felt Brown's opposition was an obsession, causing him to follow such a foolhardy scheme that ended up in death for ten of the raiders, including his sons, and ultimately his own death by hanging.

A drawing of Brown depicting him leading his men hung on the wall. His arm was raised, and his long hair and beard flew out wildly. But what caught Maggie's attention most were his eyes, which almost glowed with zeal in the black and white depiction. Apparently it caught Holly's attention also.

"Do you think he was, you know, a little crazy?" Holly asked.

"He was certainly a fanatic," the guide answered. "But

the mood of the times added plenty of pull to his own leanings. Perhaps a few decades from now someone will ask if the Vietnam War protestors and flag burners were a little crazy."

"Huh?" Holly said.

"I'll explain in the car," Maggie murmured. She thanked the guide, then said to Holly, "I think we'd better head back. It looks like a storm coming."

"See what I mean," Holly complained, as she buckled herself in. "There's so much I don't know. You went to college. You knew what the guide was talking about. I bet there's nothing you'd ever have to say 'huh' to."

Maggie laughed. "At seventeen I thought I knew just about everything. Four years of college taught me just how much I still had to learn."

One thing she still had to learn was who killed Lori Basker. Was she getting any closer, she wondered? Holly thought she was on the wrong track suspecting Rob. Was she? Should she be looking at Eric Semple more? But why was Holly so evasive about him? Then there was the waiter, Chuck. Had his teeneage obsession for Lori grown out of control? Did he decide if he couldn't have her, no one would?

Something else nagged at the back of her mind. If I was so smart I'd figure out what that was too, Maggie sighed. If only I could translate it all into an equation. This person equals x plus two. That one equals y minus five. Add it up, multiply and divide, and voilà! The murderer!

Chapter Eighteen

Maggie glanced at her watch and stepped on the gas a little harder. Holly needed to change to her uniform and be ready to work in fifteen minutes. They pulled onto the steep, winding road, and as Maggie came to the spot of her near-accident, she looked over at the scraped and dented guardrail. Her muscles tensed, and Maggie felt her heart beating faster. She bit at her lip, hard. Holly, noticing, asked, "Hey, what's the matter?"

"I almost went through that rail yesterday. Someone in a blue van—a Highview van, I believe—tried to slam me through it and down the mountain."

"Holy . . .! You could have been killed!"

Maggie turned to her. "Yes, I could have. That's why this person has to be stopped. He's killed before, and will try to kill again."

Holly said nothing, her face troubled. They rode the rest of the way in silence, until Maggie finally pulled up to a

140

side entrance of the hotel to let Holly out. She wriggled out, then, holding the door open, leaned back in.

"Thanks for everything," she said, and before Maggie could answer, closed the door and dashed off as quickly as her high heels would let her.

Maggie watched her for a moment, then drove on to park her car. She had to brake suddenly to avoid running into Tyler and Travis, the tow-headed twins she had seen twice before with Rob. They were kicking a soccer ball around on the gravel—did they ever sit still?—and had dashed out from between two parked cars. Maggie waved them across, then looked around automatically for Rob. No sign of him.

She had parked and climbed out of her car when the soccer ball came skidding toward her. She quickly blocked it with her foot to keep it from disappearing under the car.

"Thanks," called Tyler. Or was it Travis? He ran up and deftly repossessed the ball with a sideways scoop of his foot, then kicked it over to his brother.

Maggie watched them thoughtfully for a moment, then leaned back against her car, waiting for them to take a break. Their flushed cheeks showed they had been playing vigorously for some time, and she didn't have long to wait. They soon slowed to a stop and sank down to rest under a nearby tree. Maggie strolled over.

"You two are pretty good at sports," she said with a smile, and they both grinned and nodded enthusiastic agreement. "Which do you like better, soccer or tennis?"

It was no contest. "Soccer!" they both shouted out together, then laughed.

"But I like tennis too," one added. "It's just that I'm not so good at it yet." The other nodded.

"Rob's a pretty good teacher, don't you think?" Maggie asked.

"Yeah, he's fun. Not like a teacher in school, or anything."

Maggie winced at that, but managed to keep smiling. "Yes, I noticed you were having a pretty good time with him yesterday morning. Remember, you ran through the tables on the patio and nearly knocked me down?"

The boys studied her cautiously, clearly wondering if she was working up to a scolding. When they saw her smile and decided she wasn't, they grinned, remembering the incident.

"What was going on? Were you playing tag?"

"Nah." They dismissed that thought instantly with a look that said tag was much too childish for them. "We were coming back with Rob after our lesson, and he stopped to get a stone or something out of his shoe."

"Where was this?" Maggie asked. "Next to the hedge?"

"Yeah. The other side of the tables, you know?"

Maggie nodded.

"Anyway, Tyler here"—Travis started giggling—"grabs Rob's hat and starts running with it."

"And then *you* grabbed it from me," his brother chimed in.

"Yeah, and you almost fell over that other guy, trying to get it back."

"What other guy?" Maggie asked.

"A guy that works here. He was pulling weeds or something next to the hedge. He's the guy Rob got so mad at that time, over in the sports building. Boy, was he yelling!"

Eric Semple! Eric had been behind the hedge too. *He* could have heard her talking to Dyna about Lori's diary.

The twins had forgotten about Maggie and were now trying to top each other by remembering some of the words Rob had used, and how many times he had used them. Maggie left without their noticing and walked slowly toward the hotel, thinking.

So Rob had stopped on the other side of the hedge, supposedly to get something out of his shoe. He could have heard her talking with Dyna. But Eric had been there too, perhaps for a much longer time. Which one had overheard her, and to which one did it matter?

Maggie left the graveled parking lot and walked onto the grass. A crew of maintenance workers came toward her, carrying buckets and tools, and she stepped out of their way. They nodded to her as they passed.

Maggie suddenly got an idea, and she headed in the direction the workers had just come from. Searching through rhododendron and mountain laurel, it only took her a minute or two to find who she was looking for: Jack was pushing a wheelbarrow through the shrubbery in the other direction, away from her.

She picked up her pace and followed him. She wasn't sure how to question him, but she was convinced he could tell her something, if he only would.

Jack came to an isolated circle of holly trees, unaware that he was being trailed, and Maggie called out to him. He stopped and turned around, wincing as he recognized her. But he waited while she caught up to him.

"Jack, I wonder if we could talk a minute?"

He sighed, and with a look of resignation put down his wheelbarrow. He mopped his face with the sleeve of his shirt.

"I'm really sorry to keep bothering you, but this is important."

"Miss, I don't see . . ." he started to protest, then gave up, listening as Maggie quickly explained.

"I heard about an incident concerning Eric Semple. I believe he got into some trouble about his work here, and when you called him on it, his mother, Burnelle, rushed to his defense and put the blame on you. Is that right?"

"Why do you want to know?"

Maggie chose her words carefully. "There's someone at this hotel who is very dangerous. I need your help in finding out who it is."

Jack looked at her. "Do I think Eric is dangerous? Isn't

that what you're looking for? You're wondering if he's the one killed that little waitress? I don't know. I don't like the guy, but I don't know if he could kill someone. I sure as heck wouldn't want him dating my daughter, if I had one, but for a whole lot of other reasons. I've never seen him or heard of him being violent, but that doesn't mean he wouldn't be. Some folks hide their dark side real well, you know?"

Maggie nodded. She knew. How many students had she had, or heard about from other teachers, who seemed like the perfect teen until evidence of their cheating, or other nastiness, came out. She sank down onto the grass next to a small holly tree, hoping Jack would follow suit. He did, pushing his barrow out of the way, and settling down not far from her. He stretched his arms over his raised knees and looked at her, his expression resigned.

"So, tell me what happened," Maggie prodded.

"Well, what you heard is right. It wasn't long after Eric started here. I knew Burnelle had been working here for a while, but I didn't realize how much influence she had with management, with Ms. Crawford. Housekeeping poking into landscaping." He shook his head. "Doesn't make much sense, except when you know how she watches over that kid of hers."

"She does, doesn't she. Has she had to rescue him from many other problems?"

Jack shook his head. "I don't know, but it wouldn't surprise me. He's just that type of kid—kinda shrewd and kinda dumb at the same time. You know?"

Maggie nodded.

Jack picked up a twig and started peeling the bark from it. "I first ran into Burnelle years ago, though she doesn't remember it."

"Where was this?"

"Some little town west of here. I was about nineteen, hitchhiking from place to place, looking for a job. She hasn't changed much, just some gray hair now, a little heavier, you know. Same with Ms. Crawford, older and heavier since I first met her. I ran into her around that time, too, not managing any hotels then, though. She's really worked her way up and brought her daughter along with her. But they're two of a kind, Crawford and the girl. Smart and tough.

"Anyway, I guess I didn't make much impression on either of them, Burnelle or Crawford, or else I've changed a lot too. Suppose I must have. I was just a teen then." Jack's face froze, and he looked away from Maggie.

"What's the matter?"

"I was just reminded of something. Something that still gives me the creeps."

"What?"

"I had hitched a ride from this guy. But we split up at a diner. He was going south. By the time I found another ride I heard about a pretty bad accident on the highway he had taken. I'm just about sure it was him. The car was completely burned up. If I had stayed with him I would have been killed."

"Pretty scary."

Jack nodded.

"So now you're working at the same place as both Burnelle and Ms. Crawford."

"Funny, isn't it? It's almost like something pulled us together here." Jack stood and grabbed the handles of his wheelbarrow.

Maggie rose too. "Thank you, Jack, for talking to me."

Jack nodded, his face somewhat bemused, as though he had surprised himself with all the words that came tumbling out, breaking through his normal reserve. Maggie wondered if she had stirred up things in his head that he preferred to leave undisturbed, but he didn't look uncomfortable, only thoughtful, like someone discovering long-forgotten items in an unused drawer.

They separated and went in different directions, Jack continuing the way he had been heading when Maggie first caught up to him, and Maggie walking back to the hotel. They were many yards apart when Maggie heard Jack calling to her.

"Miss! Miss!"

She turned, barely able to hear him across the distance.

"She had the kid then, just a baby then," he said. "But she didn't like to talk about it."

"Who, Jack? Who do you mean?"

"At the diner. She didn't want to talk about it."

"Which one, Burnelle or Ms. Crawford?" Maggie called again, but Jack was too far away, and he disappeared now, into thick shrubbery.

Maggie was on the verge of going after him when she heard the twins calling to each other as they ran from the parking lot toward the hotel.

"Are you sure that was Rob?" one was asking.

"I think. Over that way. Someone with a blue shirt like his. C'mon, maybe we can catch up to him."

Was Rob nearby? Maggie suddenly didn't want him to see her questioning hotel employees. She turned back to the hotel and in a moment saw the twins rushing by in a blur. There wasn't any sign of Rob ahead of them, but she continued on, confident that she could catch Jack at another time.

Back in her room Maggie sat staring out the window. The sun glinted on the mountains, highlighting their intricate shapes. Closer by, flowers showed off their stunning colors against grass that was lush and green. But her thoughts were not on the beauty before her. They moved restlessly over her recent conversations with the twins and with Jack, gradually shifting from Burnelle, Kathryn Crawford, and Eric, to Rob. They lingered on Rob.

Jack had mentioned the hidden dark side some people

had. Did Rob have a dark side? He had explained away the rumors of violence at Wimbledon, but then he had lied to her almost immediately about keeping his lesson with Mr. Anderson at ten o'clock, the same time she was being menaced by the blue van. Had he lied to her about the rest? Maggie didn't like that thought, but knew she had to pursue it, examine it. Her feelings didn't matter. She couldn't let them matter. Facts mattered.

And now she had evidence of Eric lurking within hearing range of her conversation with Dyna. He must have overheard her talking about Lori's journal. What had he done about it, if anything? But that waiter, Chuck, she remembered, had certainly seen the journal. He almost soaked it, could have destroyed it by tipping her water glass. And Maggie saw him talking to Ms. Crawford soon after. Telling her about the journal?

The phone rang and Maggie jumped. Her brother's familiar voice coming through the receiver broke through her tension and made her smile. His tone, though, was not happy.

"Why are you still there, Maggie?" he demanded.

"Hi, Joe, how are you?"

"Don't 'Hi, Joe' me. Maggie, you promised you'd get out of there."

"Don't put words into my mouth, Joe. I never promised anything. I've had things to do here. I'll leave when I'm finished."

"Things to do? What? What are you talking about?"

"I think I'm getting close to finding out who killed Lori."

"*You're* getting close? What do you think you're doing? You're not the police."

"The police don't seem to be doing much at all. They seem to be waiting for some drifter to walk into their office and say 'Hi, I'm the one who did it.' Lori's parents deserve better than that. How can they rest until they know the truth, until they get justice?"

"What about *our* parents, Maggie? Mom's worried enough just thinking about you being off somewhere alone. How do you think she'll feel when she finds out about all this?"

"Someday Mom—and Dad—are going to have to face the fact that I'm all grown up. I'm sorry it's been so hard for them." The thought of Burnelle's overprotectiveness flashed through Maggie's mind, and she gritted her teeth. "Just keep them out of this for now. Look, Joe, if you'd do something for me, it'd be a big help and I might be able to finish and come home soon." Maggie knew if she dangled that carrot in front of Joe he'd jump for it.

"What can I do?"

"Go to a library, one that has old newspapers on microfiche, and look up something for me." She explained what she needed. She could hear Joe scratching away with a pencil, taking it all down. She could almost envision him leaping into the family car and screeching onto the highway heading for the library. Good old Joe. Her dear baby brother who felt he had to look after her, and would probably be up here dragging her out of her room if he thought it would work. She hoped he would find what she wanted, but in the meantime it would keep him out of her hair.

He had struck a chord, mentioning her parents. Maggie knew quite well just what they would go through when they finally found out all she had been up to. She hated putting them through anything stressful, but knew she had to live her life for herself now, not only for them. Her decisions were her own, and she would take the consequences for them, whatever they might be.

The phone rang again, and Maggie picked it up, half expecting to hear Joe's voice. Instead it was Charles, from the front desk.

"Miss Olenski, I'm afraid I have some bad news. There's been some damage done to your car."

Chapter Nineteen

Maggie burst from the elevator into the hotel lobby. Her eyes darted around, thoughts racing, and she caught sight of Dyna blinking at her with surprise from the magazine stand. Maggie called out a quick, "Come on," and Dyna dropped a copy of *People* and followed without a word, the two of them half-running through the hallways that led to the side door. Maggie slammed the door open and they exited into the parking lot, slowing as they approached Maggie's last parking spot, shock spreading on both faces.

"Oh, Maggie. Your poor car!" Dyna cried. Maggie stared, unable to say anything, the pain of what she saw taking her breath away.

A large rock lay on the backseat of Maggie's car, having made its way through the back window, which now had a gaping hole and spider webs of cracks and splinters. Several large and small shards of glass lay next to the rock and on the floor of the car.

"Who could have done it?" Dyna asked.

149

Charles came up next to them, having left his post at the desk, and followed quickly behind. He looked equally mournful, seeming to take this almost as personally as Maggie. "We have no idea," he said, shaking his head. "A guest noticed it on his way in and reported it to us. I can't say how sorry I am about this, Miss."

Maggie nodded. Several thoughts and feelings coursed through her, not the least of which was a quickly growing anger at the person who had done this. She circled the car, looking at the damage from all angles.

"Nobody saw or heard anything when this happened?" she asked.

"Apparently not. We've asked around a bit, but the kitchen staff was busy setting up for dinner, the maintenance crew had quit for the day, and that lone guest was the only one passing through, after the fact."

"Very convenient. Someone certainly knows exactly when to strike."

"Let me make a few phone calls, Miss. The sheriff should be notified. And management should be told. This sort of thing should not happen at our hotel." He paused, and Maggie knew they were all thinking of Lori. Another, more terrible incident that shouldn't have happened there. Charles coughed, continuing, "At least we can arrange for the repairs."

"Thank you, Charles. That's very kind."

Charles hurried off, and Maggie ran a finger along a deep scratch in the paint which ran nearly front to back along the driver's side of her car. "This wasn't from the guardrail. Whoever threw that rock took the time to scratch the car first."

"But why?" Dyna asked.

"It's all a grim message. They might as well have scratched the words into the paint: 'Go home, Maggie. Get out of here.' "

"Maybe you should," Dyna said softly.

Maggie just looked at her. "I must be getting close, Dyna. Someone is very worried."

"Someone also has the advantage, Maggie. They know who you are, and *where* you are, but you don't know who they are."

"I mean for that to change."

It wasn't long before the sheriff's car pulled up, quietly, with no lights flashing. This was no emergency. In fact, Maggie was surprised he would take the time to investigate it at all. But the deputy was all business, touching his hat politely as he greeted them, and writing down all he could see and that she could tell him about the damage done to her car.

A small crowd had gathered by this time, attracted by the presence of the official car. Maggie caught a glimpse of Holly peering from the side door, wearing her uniform and holding an empty tray. Her face was distressed, but she didn't come out to look closer, or to talk to Maggie.

The twins, Tyler and Travis, showed up, in bathing suits with towels wrapped around their necks, stepping gingerly with their bare feet on the gravel. Maggie went up to them, the deputy following.

"Hey, guys, did you happen to be around when this happened?"

Their eyes grew big. "It wasn't us, honest! We were kicking the soccer ball around, but we headed back onto the grass and away from here. We didn't break your window!"

"I know. It wasn't your ball that broke it." Maggie explained to the deputy that the boys had been near the parking lot as she left it. "Somebody hurled a heavy rock through the window. I just wondered if you saw anyone hanging around that looked like he might have that on his mind?"

The twins looked at each other and shrugged. "We didn't see anyone like *that*."

"After I left you I heard one of you calling out that you saw Rob. Was he coming this way?"

"Rob? No, I thought I saw him going toward the pool, but when we got there we couldn't find him. We were hot, so we decided to get our suits on and go swim."

Maggie knew Rob was probably the last person they would want to tattle on, but she could read in their faces that they were telling the truth.

The deputy said, "If you think of anything that would help us, let me know," and handed them his card. They took it solemnly, as if it were their own personal Junior G-Man badge, and nodded in unison.

"We're not going to find out who did it for now," Maggie said, as they walked back to her car. "But I am sure it was the same person who drove a blue van and tried to kill me out on the road, and the same person who killed Lori Basker."

The deputy didn't comment, but looked at her with a grim face. He entered something in his notebook, then flipped it closed. "I'll need to go in and talk to the front desk man, and the guest who reported this. We'll be in touch." Before he turned to go, Maggie noticed him glance up in the direction of the hotel side door. Holly was gone, and Maggie saw the waiter, Chuck, standing in her place. To her surprise, he and the deputy seemed to lock eyes for a moment. Was she imagining it? If not, what did it mean?

"Maggie, now what?" Dyna stood at her side, agitated and nearly plucking at her sleeve.

The deputy had left, and the side doorway was now vacant. Maggie shook her head. "I don't know."

The crowd had wandered away, and Maggie and Dyna strolled off toward the pool.

"It's no coincidence that a rock was used for both this vandalism and for killing Lori."

"Yeah, I was thinking about that," Dyna said. "Another message?"

"Possibly. A convenient weapon, also. No fingerprints on the rough surface, no need to dispose of it, easy to find around here, I'm sure."

"Would it take a lot of strength, do you think?"

"Not to heave it through my car window. The right distance, right angle, and the weight of the rock would do the rest. As for killing Lori, I don't know. I'd think you'd need strength along with the element of surprise. But perhaps the anger the killer felt toward Lori would generate enough force."

Dyna shivered. "How could anyone feel enough anger toward the kind of girl you described to crash a rock into her head?"

"That's the question. And what caused that anger."

They came up to the pool and saw the twins dive in, pop up, then splash each other, all worries such as Maggie and Dyna had obviously absent from their thoughts. Maggie envied them, remembering the hopes she had had for a peaceful vacation not too long ago.

"Miss?"

Maggie turned and saw Burnelle hurrying toward her from the hotel's patio doors.

"Miss Crawford asked me to tell you the garage will be sending someone to fix your car first thing in the morning. They promise it can be done in a few hours."

Maggie looked toward the glass doors and saw Kathryn Crawford behind them, standing stiffly near the desk. She was probably angry at another disruption in the smooth operation of her hotel, Maggie thought. And possibly angry at *me*, although I sure didn't want this any more than she did. She turned back to Burnelle. "That'll be great. Thanks."

"Such a shame," Burnelle added, her expression concerned. "But at least no one was hurt."

"Yes, but I'd like to know who did it."

Burnelle was silent, her lips pressed together tightly as though trying to keep words from spilling out. She wrung her hands. Finally, as though coming to a decision, she blurted out, "That tennis fellow? I didn't actually see him do anything, but I happened to see him leaving the parking lot just about that time. I didn't know anything had happened to your car, so I didn't think anything about it. I was just catching a breath of air away from the hot kitchen.

"I know he didn't see me, and please don't tell him I said anything. I, I'd hate to think of what he might do. And I really didn't see him do anything. But he looked all flushed, and he was walking fast, brushing his hands together as though they had gotten dirty. I thought you should know." Burnelle's own face was flushed now, and she looked acutely uncomfortable. Before Maggie could say anything she spun around and rushed back into the hotel.

"Rob," Dyna murmured, as they both stared after her.

Maggie didn't say anything. Her eyes were on the door through which Burnelle had disappeared.

"I knew it. I knew it." Dyna's face lit up. "Remember Lori's journal? You said she mentioned 'R.' Who else? It had to be him."

Something caught Maggie's eye and she looked to the right, across the lawn to the path leading to the tennis courts. A tall, slim man—it could have been Rob, but she couldn't tell from the distance and shadows—was walking away from them. Suddenly he stopped and turned around— he appeared to be looking right at them.

That evening, Maggie sat waiting on a wooden bench just beyond the pool, overlooking the large expanse of lawn. She had chosen that bench because it had no shrubs or structures nearby where anyone could lurk, overhearing. The precaution, in light of recent events, seemed necessary. She sat waiting for Holly to meet her, on her break.

Holly had stopped at their table to refill the water glasses when Maggie and Dyna were having dinner, and had whispered to Maggie that she wanted to talk to her later. Maggie agreed and, after Holly had moved away, told Dyna she thought it might be about Eric Semple.

"On our excursion today after the funeral, we talked about a lot of things. But whenever I tried to probe more deeply about Eric, Holly clammed up. After what's happened, I have a feeling she may be ready to open up."

Dyna shook her head. "What could Eric's connection be to all this?" She still apparently zeroed in on Rob as the only possible murderer.

"That's what I need to find out. He's been lurking around this whole business very suspiciously."

"Maybe Rob is trying to make it look like Eric's guilty— you know, to cover his own tracks. Or maybe they're somehow working together."

Maggie had considered that, but remained unsure. Was she letting her own feelings get in the way of her objectivity? She hoped not. On the bench now, she looked at her watch: eight. That's when Holly said she could take her break. The sky was still light, but a soft, sleepy light, with some dark clouds gathering off to the west. Maggie heard an owl hooting somewhere in the trees.

She heard distant voices and the clanking of pots as the kitchen door opened. Soon she saw Holly's small, slim form hurrying over the grass in her uniform and white sneakers, her dark hair a bouncing cloud around her head. She plopped down on the bench next to Maggie, immediately pulled out a cigarette, lit up, and drew on it.

"Sorry if I'm late. That new guy, Chuck—they hired him to replace Lori, you know? He said he's waited tables before, but he's been mixing up orders all night and I've had to bail him out. Well, never mind. Burnelle saw me take off and she's probably set her stopwatch, so I better get down to business."

Maggie waited quietly while Holly drew once more on her cigarette. Finally she glanced over at Maggie and began. "Well, I was thinking, ever since I got back today. About what you said, that this person who killed Lori's got to be stopped, and how you almost got killed yourself yesterday. And then seeing what somebody did to your car. It all really got to me.

"I've been holding back. I don't know why. Just being stupid, as usual. But I'm thinking it's about time I used my head a little, you know? Anyway, you were asking about Eric, and I wasn't giving you straight answers. He's not such an okay guy. He's a real lowlife."

Maggie wasn't surprised, but she waited for Holly to go on.

"He's been stealing from the hotel, big-time. I guess I felt guilty 'cause a lot of us knew about it but didn't say anything."

"What sort of things has he been stealing?"

"Oh, it started out with little things. I guess that's why nobody said anything, 'cause it just didn't seem worth it, you know? Like, this is a big hotel, and who's going to care if some garden clippers are missing, or there's only nineteen instead of twenty holly bushes to plant. But then he moved up to bigger things. Electronic stuff he could sell, some things from the guests. He'd brag about how smart he was about it, only picking guests who seemed distracted or vague about how much cash they still had in their wallets, or where they might have left their jewelry."

"Did many of you know about this?" Maggie asked.

"Not a lot. There were a few of us who were friends with him at the beginning, when he first started working here. You know, going for a beer once in a while. But then we began keeping our distance when he started bragging a lot about what he did. He knew we couldn't say anything by then without getting ourselves into trouble, but it was getting too weird."

Maggie controlled her growing excitement as she asked the next question. "Holly, did Lori know what Eric was doing?"

Holly frowned, thinking hard. She puffed at her cigarette one last time, then threw it down and ground it under her foot. She looked at Maggie. "I remember once he came in the kitchen when things were slow and showed me a watch he had just grabbed from someone's bag while they were soaking in the jacuzzi. Lori was there, in the kitchen. She didn't say anything, but I remember the look on her face. Rick thought she was impressed, that's how dumb he was. But she wasn't impressed. She was upset."

Maggie grabbed Holly's arm. "What did you just call him? Rick?"

Holly looked at her, puzzled. "Yeah. That's what most of us call him, I guess. Why?"

"Most of you? Did that include Lori? Did she call him Rick?"

"Lori? Yeah, she met him through us, so I guess she did. Yeah, she called him Rick."

Maggie hurried up to her room, feeling both elated and frightened. She had found a motive. Eric Semple, who had means and opportunity, also had a motive. He could have killed Lori for his own protection. If Eric was the "R" Lori refered to in her journal, perhaps she had tried to talk him into giving up his life of thievery. And when she realized that wasn't going to happen, he could have feared she would turn him in and killed her. He also could have overheard her, Maggie, talking about Lori's diary, and tried to stop Maggie from getting to the sheriff with it.

Realizing all that, putting it all together, brought on much of the elation. But she was aware too, that part of her excitement came from the hope that this eliminated Rob from suspicion. She could admit that fully now, to herself. She had a strong attraction to Rob, and was almost sure he felt the same about her. They had much more to learn about each other—the relationship had a lot of growing to do—but now, perhaps, a major obstacle had been dissolved.

The fear she also felt, though, came from the fact of Lori's murderer taking on flesh and blood. He was no longer just a shadowy figure in her mind. He was real. And he was here.

Maggie shivered and fit the key card into her door. She intended to call Dyna to come over, to talk it over with her. As she stepped into the room, however, her foot crunched a piece of paper on the floor. A note had been slipped under the door. Maggie picked it up and read the message which had been scrawled on hotel stationery:

MAGGIE—I HAVE SOMETHING UNDERLINE IMPORTANT TO SHOW YOU! AT THE TENNIS COURTS. COME MEET ME THERE RIGHT AWAY.

                                                                        DYNA

"Dyna! No!" Maggie gasped in horror. Would Dyna really be so foolish as to go to the tennis courts alone at this time of day? She looked at the window, at the rapidly darkening sky, and wanted to believe she wouldn't. But she knew Dyna was an impulsive, emotions-over-thought person, and feared the worst. Maggie whirled around, shoving the note into her pocket, and rushed out the door. She had to get to her friend before anything terrible happened.

She punched the elevator button and bounced impatiently, waiting for only a second, then turned and slammed through the stairway door, running down the stairs as rapidly as she could. She still wore her funeral clothes, which included dress-flat shoes, not running shoes, and she had to hold onto the rail to keep from slipping on the smooth, uncarpeted surface.

She reached the ground floor and faced an exit door, pushed it open, and stopped a moment to get her bearings.

The door let her out at the left side of the hotel, farthest from the restaurant and kitchen. The pool was to her right, and the woods and tennis courts straight ahead. She looked around quickly for any sign of Dyna, hoping that perhaps she hadn't gotten that much of a head start, but her hopes sank when she didn't see the familiar, tousled blond head among the few stray guests. Maggie took off for the path to the courts.

Why did Dyna go off alone? she cried to herself. What could have been so important that she couldn't wait? She felt a drop or two of the rain that had been threatening earlier, and slowed to catch her breath as she finally stepped into the woods on the mulched path.

Her eyes strained to see in the dim light, still hoping to catch up with her friend, but the path took so many turns that she couldn't see any great distance ahead. She thought of calling out, but an inner caution warned her not to advertise her presence too much. She hurried along, dodging branches hidden by shadows as best she could, slowly becoming enveloped in the deep silence of the woods.

She had just taken a turn that showed more light up ahead, indicating she was close to the open space of the tennis area, when she heard a rustle in the trees next to her. Snapping her head to the left she saw a form step out of the darkness, and her breath caught in her chest. It was Eric Semple.

"Teacher," he said, as he stepped close to her. No toothpick dangled from his lips now. Maggie looked back at him, frozen. "What's your hurry, hmm?" He grinned and stood only inches from her now. Maggie wondered wildly if calling for help would do any good. Was Dyna within hearing distance? Was anyone?

"Cat got your tongue?"

Maggie backed away from him, slowly. "What do you want?"

"Gosh, I'm just out for a nice evening stroll, like you,"

he answered, smirking. "Thought maybe we could take it together, you know, arm in arm."

"I . . . I'm meeting someone. I'm late."

"Teacher! I'm shocked. Now what would your principal say if he knew you were meeting someone in the woods."

"It'd be none of his business, just as it's none of yours." Some of Maggie's fear subsided as her anger rose. She began to think Eric was simply up to his same stupid teasing. After all, he couldn't know what she had just found out about him. She started to walk away.

Eric grabbed her arm. "Hold on . . ." and Maggie turned to face him defiantly, to shake him off. Suddenly she heard a sound behind her and her hopes leaped up that help had come. She didn't have a chance to find out. The last things she saw were Eric's eyes widening as he looked past her. Then something rock-hard struck her head, lights exploded behind her eyes, and everything went black.

Chapter Twenty

Consciousness surfaced for a moment, and Maggie became aware of pain, motion, the musty smell of something covering her, and murmuring voices. She struggled to stay on that surface, to remember what had happened and think of where she was. Then she began bouncing and rocking, her sore head bumping against something hard, and blackness descended again.

When she next awoke, she was lying on something hard and cold, the smelly cover was gone, and pain had spread throughout her body. It was dark and still. She strained her eyes and her ears. Slowly she made out the outlines of a few large, dark shapes. And she heard a faint hissing sound.

She tried to move and found she couldn't. Her hands were tied behind her back, and her ankles tied together. Trussed like a chicken, she thought, aware of the ridiculousness, but she didn't feel much like laughing. She struggled, however, to pull herself into a sitting position. It took several minutes of effort, interrupted by waves of dizziness and pain. Sweat broke out on her face, but it quickly evaporated into the chilly air. Maggie's stomach churned, adding to her misery, and she took several deep breaths, trying to control it.

She sat up for several minutes, waiting for the dizziness to gradually diminish, then concentrated on focusing her eyes in the dark. Little by little she could see more of her surroundings, and she realized she was in an old barn. She could see slits of light, or rather of lesser darkness, between the boards that formed the walls. She couldn't make out the large, indistinct shapes around her. There were odors of moldy hay and dampness, oil and old wood. She listened carefully and realized the hissing sound she heard was rain. The storm she had seen coming had arrived, covering any tracks of her abduction, she thought dismally.

Something skittered against her leg, and she jerked her feet back sharply, almost knocking herself off balance and back down to a prone position. She fought hard to stay upright and also to keep down feelings of panic. *Think, Maggie, think*, she ordered herself. Panic later, when there's time. You're alive, for now. Concentrate on keeping yourself that way.

Easy for you to say, she answered herself. But to fight the rising panic she started quietly reciting the postulates of Euclid, something she had had her geometry students do countless times. "Postulate one: It is possible to draw a straight line from any point to any point. Postulate two: It is possible . . ." It began to work. By the time she ran through them all she had calmed down considerably and was able to focus her thoughts.

How did I get here? was her first question. She thought hard, remembering facing Eric on the path, then a sharp blow on her head followed by blankness, broken briefly when she heard voices and felt motion. I must have been riding in something then, a truck or a van. One of the blue vans?

But Eric wasn't the one who hit her, she realized. She had been facing him when it happened, and was hit from behind. And *he was looking past me*, she remembered. *He had looked surprised. So who came up behind me? And whose was the other voice I heard later?*

Could it have been Rob? she wondered. Waves of a new kind of pain washed over her. *Could Rob have been working with Eric, stealing from the hotel, perhaps to raise money for his own tennis operation? Or was talk of his future dream all just a lie? Was the story about his fight with the former girlfriend just another cover?*

Maybe his anger and shouting at Eric had been over stolen goods? Or maybe the anger was another cover-up? Questions without answers raced through her mind. Something, though, was missing. She couldn't seem to shake her head clear enough to think of it right now. It hurt too much.

She didn't have the time to spend searching for it either. She was here, alone and alive for now. That could change at any moment. Obviously, the two who had put her here planned to return, to dispose of her at a more convenient time, when alibis had been arranged. How soon that would be she had no way of knowing and therefore needed to work on her escape immediately.

Suddenly she remembered Dyna. *Where was Dyna? Had she been attacked as Maggie had? Was she alive?* Horrifying visions of her friend swirled before her eyes. Maggie felt herself starting to lose it again, and did another rapid recitation. "Common notion one: Things which are equal to the same thing are also equal to one another." By the time she got to "Five: The whole is greater than the part," she was again calm. And thinking more clearly.

It was possible, she now realized, that Dyna hadn't written that note at all. Maggie could have been lured to the woods by her attacker. Foolish as that made her feel, she sincerely hoped that was true, and that Dyna was safely in her room right now, watching TV or sound asleep.

"Dyna?" Maggie whispered fearfully, then raised her voice to call again. "Dyna? Are you here?" There was no answer, and Maggie wasn't sure if that made her feel better or worse.

She struggled with her bonds. They didn't feel overly tight. Possibly whoever tied them was in a hurry or thought she would stay unconscious. However, wiggling and twisting her hands as much as she could still didn't loosen the ropes enough to release her.

What were her chances of finding something sharp to cut the ropes on, here in the dark? Memory of the skittery thing came to her, and the thought of sliding around touching everything she came across brought shivers. However, thoughts of the alternative, to sit and wait for someone to come back and kill her moved her to action, and she struggled to get herself on her feet.

She couldn't do it. The combination of the ropes and her dizziness kept her from getting enough balance to stand upright. She needed something to brace herself.

Maggie slid, inch by inch, along the packed dirt floor as best she could, pushing with her feet and sliding back with her hips. After several minutes and much effort, she managed to reach the closest wall, breathing heavily, and pushed herself tightly against it. At first it seemed to take more strength than she had, but slowly she got her feet under her, and she started to rise up, bit by bit. She was almost halfway up when her feet, still in the leather-soled flat shoes, slipped and flew out from under her. She landed on her backside with a painful thump. Her head swam and throbbed, and she waited for it to clear, fighting back tears of frustration.

She tried again. This time, by getting her feet more firmly under her and digging the edges of her shoes into the dirt, she managed to keep her footing, and in a few minutes she was upright. Panting and sweating from the effort, she waited, resting and thinking of what to do next.

She knew she couldn't leave the wall or she'd fall. She decided to move along it, using a combination of small foot movements and hops, aiming for the closest dark shape in hopes it might be something with a sharp edge. She came to a corner, and as she worked her way around, her face hit a large cobweb and she let out a screech, jerking back, sputtering and rubbing her face on her shoulders. Without hands she couldn't get it all off, so she tried her best to forget it and not think about spiders crawling in her hair.

She also hoped there was no one outside the barn to hear her yelp. The rain made that less likely. If she were being guarded, they would certainly be indoors, not out, and would have made their presence known by now.

When she finally reached the dark shape she had seen from her starting point, her disappointment was keen. It was only an old wooden table. No pointed edges and no handy knives sitting on it within reach. From the feel of the dust and grit on it, it hadn't been touched by anyone for quite a while. This barn must be forgotten and unused for years, she thought, an ideal place for stashing inconveniently nosy investigators.

Joe was right. She should have left the hotel right away. This wasn't at all like the things she used to get into when they were kids. The combination of her disappointment with the table and the thought of Joe brought tears to her eyes, but she blinked them away and swallowed several times. No time for that. Tears later—work now.

Maggie returned to her slow, painful inching along the wall. She was just starting to get into a smooth rhythm when something jabbed her leg. Something pointy, but not sharp enough to break her skin. She bent down slowly to feel it with her hands. It was the head of a large nail jutting out of a wooden barn slat. She tugged at it, but it was seated firmly, perhaps about half its length.

Maggie sank down on her knees, and moved her ropes over the nailhead. Perhaps she could loosen and untie the knots by hooking the nail through them somehow? With her hands tied behind her, it all had to be done by touch. She pictured her abductors coming back for her and started to panic again, thinking this was impossible, there wasn't enough time, then pushed those thoughts away and concentrated on the task.

She tried it over and over again, feeling the nail slide over the ropes, failing to catch a loop, controlling her frustration. After dozens of attempts, she was close to giving up, but finally the nail caught. She could feel the knot slowly pull open, just a little. The nail slipped out, but she was able to catch it back in again. The loop grew bigger. Again and again she worked at it, and gradually her efforts were rewarded. First one loop, then another, and finally the ropes pulled loose from her wrists. She had done it!

Maggie quickly turned to the ropes around her ankles and had them untied in moments. She rubbed her ankles and her wrists, exulting, then rose and crept to the door. All she could hear was the soft, steady fall of rain. She peered through several cracks and saw no truck or van, and no human shapes.

Maggie's impulse was to get out of there fast, but instead she turned back to the inside of the barn. She had to make sure her friend really wasn't there before she left.

She felt her way slowly around the remaining walls and through the inner section of the barn, now able to use her hands, checking carefully in the dark for a human shape, listening for any human sound.

Maggie stumbled over bits of wood and came upon one large dark object she tentatively identified as a rusty field tiller. She found a dried and crackling tarp which covered nothing but dirt, and scraped her skin on a couple of old broken barrels and baskets. She examined every inch of the place before she returned to the door, satisfied finally that she was indeed alone.

She checked the outdoor area again through the cracks.

There were no signs of life. Her eyes and ears told her it was safe to venture out. But in her shaken state of mind it still took all her courage to open the barn door and step outside. She couldn't overcome the feeling that any moment something would come crashing down on her head, or strong hands would grab her.

When they didn't, and she was outside the barn, rain falling on her face and only the dark shapes of trees to be seen nearby, Maggie took a deep breath, turned toward the trees, and ran.

She had been walking for hours, it seemed. The barn she had escaped from was apparently out in the middle of nowhere. She saw no lights, no houses, only endless fields and trees. She had no way of knowing if she had been wandering in circles, possibly missing a lifesaving road by only yards. At least the rain had now stopped, but she was still soaked and shivering, and she had more than once stepped out of one of her flat shoes as it stuck in mud, having then to search for it in the dark.

She felt herself coming close to exhaustion, and had to fight the impulse to curl up against a tree and sleep. After the first thirty minutes or so, she had stopped looking back fearfully for pursuers, stopped listening for running feet or the sound of a motor. Her only concern now was finding help.

As she trudged, pushing herself step by step over acres of field, she thought of Lori's murder, going over all the information she had found out, and slowly discovering things she had overlooked. Missing pieces became visible, one by one, and a picture began to take shape in her mind. The moon slowly edged out from behind concealing clouds, shining its light in hidden corners, and Maggie felt the truth edging out similarly, bit by bit.

Gradually, she realized who had attacked her in the woods, and who had killed Lori, and who had probably killed the other two Highview workers. It was not with any feeling of triumph, however, that she came to her conclusion, but rather with a feeling of deep sadness. She almost wished she didn't know. Almost.

Maggie came to a cornfield and, skirting it, found herself suddenly on a narrow road. Although her hopes rose that she might now be able to flag down a motorist, none appeared, and the only sounds she heard were the chirps of crickets and tree frogs.

She followed the road for a while, limping now on sore, bleeding feet, hugging herself for warmth. Coming over a hill, she saw a small building up ahead, its white walls reflecting the moonlight. Excitement leaped up until she realized the building was totally dark, obviously vacant. Still, something about it seemed hopeful as her memory stirred. Something looked familiar.

She was staring at it as she walked closer, searching for any signs of life, when a dark shape, about the size and height of a small car, caught her eye to the right, in a clearing several feet from the road.

Maggie stopped, first startled, then puzzled, trying to identify the shape. It appeared, at first, to be a fallen tree, lying at about a thirty-degree angle to the ground, but with no sprouting branches. There were two round shapes at its low end, wheel-like. What was it? She took a few tentative steps toward it, then suddenly laughed and ran the rest of the way over to it. She ran a hand over its painted surface and rested a cheek against it.

A cannon. It was a Civil War cannon. She was at Antietam.

She turned toward the white building. Dunker Church. The first stop on the driving tour she had taken this same day. That meant she wasn't very far from the visitors' center. It must be right there, beyond that cluster of trees up ahead. With the pay phone out front. She could call for help! Maggie was so happy she nearly wept. Instead, she limped back to the road and put her remaining ounce of energy into walking those last few yards to rescue.

The low-lying visitors' center came into view, and Maggie saw the phone, its gentle light illuminating the numbered buttons that would connect her to the rest of the world. She thought she had never seen anything more beautiful. She picked up her pace, stumbling and staggering by now, and finally reached it, pulled the receiver up to her ear, and punched in three numbers: 9-1-1.

"Sheriff's office, please," she said quietly, her voice husky with exhaustion. When the crisp voice came on the line, Maggie told her story, condensing it at much as possible but all the time thinking how wild and fantastic it must sound. The reaction she got was not disbelief, however, but a promise of immediate action. Of rescue. She sighed with relief. "Thank you."

Maggie sagged against the sides of the telephone enclosure. She closed her eyes, and permitted herself a moment of rest. It was over. Then she corrected herself.

It was almost over.

Chapter Twenty-one

Tree frogs chirped noisily to each other in the otherwise silent woods, and the moon cast long, eerie shadows of the trees around the old barn. Maggie and the sheriff waited inside the barn, with deputies scattered behind trees and shrubs beyond, cars hidden and flashlights off. From her description, they had been able, after a false start or two, to locate the barn, and if there had been any doubts that they had found the right one, the presence of the ropes that had so recently bound Maggie erased them.

Now they hoped to catch her would-be murderers as they returned to the scene, expecting Maggie to be docilely waiting, unconscious and tied up. The sheriff had called his contact at the hotel and found out that Eric had recently been seen driving away in a pickup. A second person was also missing from the hotel area, as was Maggie's Dodge Shadow. Since Maggie had not actually seen her second attacker, it was essential to let them both incriminate themselves in front of witnesses.

"Good work, Chuck, Thanks," the sheriff had said into the phone, and Maggie's eyes had widened.

"Is that Chuck, the waiter? The one who knew Lori in high school?"

"That's right." The sheriff set his car phone down and climbed out of the car with a soft groan. "He's also my nephew. Studying law enforcement over at the university. I asked him to help us out by working at the hotel this summer, keeping his eyes open. We've had our suspicions about that place for a while now, but didn't have any hard evidence."

Maggie nodded with a straight face, hiding her surprise. So the sheriff had not been as inactive as she thought. And Chuck, who had been one of her suspects, was the sheriff's nephew! She wondered if Chuck had been watching her in turn, perhaps suspecting her as she suspected him?

The sound of a motor came faintly through the woods, and the tree frogs fell silent. Tension in Maggie and, she was sure, the other watchers rose as faculties were strained to their limit, listening, waiting, poised for action. The sheriff had first insisted that Maggie stay behind, safely in one of the cars, but she would have none of it.

"I'll stay out of your way," she had insisted. "But I've come this far, and I must see the finish, to see if I'm right."

"I have to say, what you told us surprised me. I was pretty sure about the kid, but had no idea about the other one." He directed Maggie to the front corner of the barn, farthest from the door. Someone had thrown a warm jacket over her shoulders, and Maggie peered through the loose boards, watching and listening.

Was she right? She had to be. All the pieces fit, even though she didn't have hard proof yet. But she was sure the proof would be there, in the newspaper files that she had sent Joe to look up, in the DNA tests that would be done, but most of all in the imminent reappearance of her abductors. Lori must have realized at least some of it, but in her trusting innocence had laid her head on the block. Maggie shivered and pulled the jacket more closely around her. Now it would be over, the killings would stop, the madness would end.

The sound of the motor grew louder, and gradually a ghostly gray pickup materialized through the trees as it bounced toward them on squeaky springs over the rough dirt and gravel road. It stopped in the small clearing before the barn, and the motor sputtered to silence. Seconds later Maggie's own dark red Shadow came up the road and stopped immediately behind the truck.

The truck's door opened, and Eric Semple stepped out and stood beside it, looking toward the barn. Maggie did not breathe. A single frog started to chirp again.

"You coming?" Eric called to the driver of the car, and for an answer the car's door opened. A large figure climbed out and stood on the ground next to the small car. Maggie sucked in her breath as the figure stepped from the shadows and into the moonlight.

Burnelle Semple had returned with her son to commit murder. And her intended victim this time was Maggie.

"Where're we gonna push her off?" Eric asked his mother. He stood by his truck and seemed in no hurry to move from it.

"Olson's Ridge. There's been plenty of accidents there before. One more won't arouse suspicion. And everyone knows she's not used to these mountain roads."

Burnelle's voice carried clearly in the still night air, and, obviously unaware that other ears beside her son's were picking it up, she spoke confidently. "She almost crashed through the guardrails just the other day, you know, and even conveniently filled out a report on it." An eerie laugh followed, and Maggie felt goose bumps rise on her skin. The exhaustion from her ordeal had long been overrun by adrenaline, and her breath came quickly as she listened and watched.

"You haul her into her car now," Burnelle directed her son, "and I'll drive it over to the ridge. You follow behind." Eric did not move.

"Can't we just do it here and leave her?" Eric's voice had taken on a reluctant, whiny tone. "Why take a chance going to the ridge? Why not—"

"No!" His mother cut him off sharply. "It has to look like an accident. Lori was a mistake. I acted rashly, afraid she would start talking to others. And it brought people poking their noses around. Including her." She jerked her head toward the barn. "This time I've planned it right, like I did the first two times, both of us having clear alibis back at the hotel when people started to notice she was missing.

"I got her car keys from her room as soon as we got back and moved her car out of sight. They'll think she went off on her own, got lost and tired, and drove off the ridge in the dark all by herself. With luck the car will catch fire and burn. Otherwise the crack on her head will look like one more injury from the accident."

"I don't know why you couldn't have just let Lori alone in the first place," Eric continued complaining. "She was okay. She wasn't hurting nothing."

"She was nosy, asking questions, noticing too much. She was close to figuring things out that would have destroyed us. She would have talked to the wrong people, and they would have taken you from me! All these years, you've been my life. I couldn't let her do that. I couldn't!"

Maggie could see Burnelle's face, and it had changed, frighteningly, from the polite hotel housekeeper she had known to a wild-eyed fanatic. The pictures of John Brown she and Holly had recently seen flashed in her mind, his face filled with righteous fury, eager to do evil for the good he believed would come from it. The Burnelle Maggie now saw, in her own righteous fury, would do anything for her perceived good of keeping her son close to her. The son who she had convinced herself was hers.

"Ma, what're you talking about? So she knew I was picking up a few things at the hotel. So what? I could have got her to keep her mouth shut. You didn't have to kill her."

"She knew! From that blood drive. She hadn't figured it all out, but she would have, with those college books of hers. And then I would have lost you! After all I went through to get you, to keep you." Burnelle's face had become grotesque, her eyes blazing wildly, madness burning in them. "You are mine. We belong together. You know that. You must know it. Together. Always. Come Eric. Come help me now, as I have been helping you."

She reached toward Eric with outstretched arms but he backed away, his face now filled with confusion, revulsion. His eyes darted around desperately, as if looking for a way to escape.

"You can hold it right there!" Sheriff Burger stepped from the barn, and deputies materialized from the surrounding woods, guns drawn. At first there was stunned silence, mother and son frozen in surprise. Then Maggie appeared, coming out of the barn and moving behind the sheriff into the moonlight.

"No!" The scream, almost a wail, came from Burnelle, and she rushed at Maggie, hands stretched forward, clawlike. The sheriff reacted instantly, knocking her to the ground and holding her there, where she writhed and shrieked, spewing forth hatred and venom. "You meddler! You serpent! Evil serpent!"

Maggie jumped back, reacting as if she had been physically struck, as though the words spouting from this fearsome, pitiful woman were pointed nails flying at her. She covered her face, then her ears, as it continued, then turned and took refuge in the barn.

The screaming continued, muffled somewhat by the closed barn door. Maggie rushed deeper inside, aware at the same time she fled from it that the barrage wasn't aimed only at her, but at a world Burnelle must have seen in her own twisted way, that she had felt always threatened her. It was as sad as it was terrible. But at least it was over. No more innocent people would be the victims of her insanity. Maggie sank down and laid her head on her knees, finally giving in to her exhaustion. An era of tragic crimes was over, she thought with relief. Lori's family might be able to move on now, and—yes, Joe, she thought with a weak smile—Maggie would finally come home.

Chapter Twenty-two

Maggie sat on her bed at the hotel, propped up against several pillows. It was very early morning, the light just breaking through the grayness of a lingering night. She had refused the suggestion of going to a hospital, asking only to be returned to her room, and Charles had summoned the doctor on call to treat her scrapes and cuts.

"Nothing serious," the doctor assured her, "but you'll probably be sore for a few days." He had wrapped a few bandages around her and given her pills, recommending that she see her own physician back in Baltimore. "You'll be going there soon?" he asked before he left.

Maggie dropped her head back against the pillows. "Yes," she said with a weary but happy smile. "Soon."

Soon! How good it would be to be back in familiar surroundings, close to those who had always cared about her and no one near who meant her harm. It seemed like an incredible luxury now, that which Maggie had lived with every day before and taken for granted, assuming it would always be the same. She realized now she had come frighteningly close to losing it all.

She thought of her parents, and how much she must mean to them. Less than twenty-four hours ago she had still felt impatient with their concern, anxious to push it some distance from her, almost careless of it. Now she knew how important it was to her, how valuable. Maggie saw the irony that their healthy parental love had nourished her life, and another's twisted, sick version of motherly love had tried to end it.

Her thoughts, along with her weariness, filled her eyes with tears, and she gave in to them, finally, letting them flow unchecked until they came no more and only a feeling of relief remained. She rested for a while, then mopped her face and mentally shook herself. Then she smiled. "Just don't think this means I'm moving back home, Mom," she said aloud. "Let's just consider this a kind of pothole on my road to independence. It may have given me a flat tire, but it's fixable and I'll soon be back in gear."

Maggie sat up with a jerk. My car! My poor car. Where is it, and has *it* survived?

Just then there was a knock on the door, and Dyna opened it and peered around the edge.

"Maggie? Maggie, are you awake?" she whispered. At Maggie's smiling nod Dyna rushed in and sat on the edge of the bed, her face anxious and her blond hair a straggling mess. Maggie saw that one crystal earring was missing.

"Are you okay?" Dyna asked, not waiting for an answer. "I saw the doctor leaving. I hardly had a chance to talk to you. I was so worried! You can't imagine what we went through when we couldn't find you."

Maggie laughed and held up a hand to stop the gush of words.

"I'm fine. What do you mean 'we.' Who else was looking for me?"

"Rob, of course!" Dyna seemed surprised that Maggie

wasn't keeping up with her. "The poor guy. I nearly attacked him when I first realized you were missing. I accused him of doing all sorts of terrible things. But then I saw the look on his face when he finally figured out what I was screaming about—I mean, the blood just drained from it! So I knew right away he was innocent."

Maggie pulled herself up. "Rob was worried?"

"Worried! He was out of his mind. It's a good thing he wasn't with you all when Burnelle and Eric came back to the barn. He would have, I don't know, done something awful."

"Really?" Maggie hugged her knees and smiled with delight.

"Uh-huh. Anyway, when we finally got word that you were safe, I asked him about the lesson thing. You know, the tennis lesson with Mr. Anderson that was canceled but Rob told you he kept, when you were being trounced by the blue van?"

"Yes?" Maggie urged, her interest intense.

"He canceled it because he was helping out Holly. He found her crying at the spot where Lori had been killed. When he tried to console her, she just got worse, saying things like how Lori was too good to die, and that it should have been her instead of Lori 'cause her life was worthless, and she was no use to anyone, and so on. I mean, she was really down.

"So Rob took her into the sports shop, canceled the lesson with Mr. Anderson, and let Holly talk it all out. He didn't tell you about it because he thought she might be embarrassed. Of course, he didn't know at the time what that led you to think."

Maggie smiled, remembering Holly's firm statement yesterday that Maggie was looking at the wrong person, that Rob was an okay guy, and knew now what had prompted that.

"And your brother, Joe, left a message last night. Something about him finding the stuff you wanted and that you might be right. What does he mean?"

Maggie's face became sober. "I asked him to do a search of old newspapers in the West Virginia and western Maryland area, the area that the gardener, Jack, told me he rode through twenty-some years ago. It was a long shot, but what he said about having met both Burnelle and Ms. Crawford around there years ago, and that one—he didn't say which—had been reluctant to talk about her baby got me thinking. I didn't have a chance to confirm it, but if it was Burnelle, that was very uncharacteristic of her. She would have been hiding something about him, and now I'm sure she had actually kidnapped him when he was a baby."

"Kidnapped!"

"Yes. And I think Lori was on the brink of proving Eric wasn't really hers."

"How?"

"That blood drive, remember? Lori probably noticed Burnelle's and Eric's blood types, and from the biology class she had recently taken noticed a problem. She wasn't an expert in genetics, but she had probably learned enough to be puzzled by it, and said something about it to Burnelle."

"About the possibility that their blood types were too far apart to be mother and son?"

"Yes, or maybe just asking what Eric's father's blood type was, to account for Eric's type. Whatever the question, it must have set Burnelle off. Thinking Lori would expose her, would bring the authorities down on her and part her from her son, Burnelle immediately silenced her."

"By killing her." Dyna's face was grim.

Maggie nodded. "You should have heard Burnelle back there at the barn. She is completely obsessed with Eric. We knew she was protective of him, but this went way beyond anything I've ever heard of. If she was sick enough to steal a baby from its parents and pretend he was her own, she was too sick to raise him as a normal mother would."

"So she killed the girl who died of an overdose of sleeping pills, and the guy who crashed his car driving back from the hotel late at night?"

"Probably. We may never know for sure, unless she confesses. They must have threatened her hold on Eric somehow. She may also have murdered the man Jack was hitching a ride with, after he found out she had Eric. Maybe by slipping sleeping pills into his food."

"And who knows how many others we don't know about?" Dyna said.

"That's right. Who knows?"

There was a knock on the door and Dyna ran to answer it. Maggie heard Rob's voice asking about her, sounding worried.

"Why don't you go in and see for yourself?" Dyna answered, stepping aside for him to enter.

He lurched through the door in a blend of hesitancy and eagerness, his eyes lighting up when he saw Maggie smiling at him. "Hi," he said. "Are you okay?"

Maggie grinned and nodded. He stood looking down at her, his face a mixture of emotions, until she held out her arms to him. He sank down into them, crushing her to him with a deep sigh. Maggie saw Dyna over his shoulder, pulling the door behind her as she tiptoed out. Maggie closed her eyes, then smiled and hugged back.

Maggie held onto Rob, loving the feel of him, the scent of him, then gently pushed him back. "Do you forgive me?" she asked.

Rob's eyes opened wide. "For what?"

"Oh, just a little thing like thinking maybe you were a murderer."

"If I had known what you were getting yourself into . . ."

"You would have what? Locked me away in an ivory tower?"

Rob grinned. "Yeah, something like that. Or maybe, you know, actually helped you."

Maggie laughed. "Oh, come on. You know you would have tried your best to talk me out of it."

"Probably. And then you would have been really convinced I was guilty. Maggie, you could have been killed!"

Maggie loved the concern she saw in his eyes. She put her hands up to his face to hold it. "I know. But I wasn't. I'm sorry for scaring everybody, but it all turned out okay." She pulled his face close and kissed him, softly at first, then harder. It turned out *very* okay, she thought as she tightened her arms around him, and felt his tighten around her. Wonderful feelings and thoughts flowed through her as they kissed, and not one of them, she realized, was a math postulate.

They were interrupted by a knock on the door.

"Maggie, the sheriff wants to talk to you," Dyna called.

Rob stood up. "I'll come back later."

"Promise?" Maggie reluctantly watched him go. Dyna, who seemed to be playing gatekeeper, let him out and ushered in the sheriff.

"Hi there, young lady," Sheriff Burger said, striding to the foot of the bed, hat in hand. Maggie noticed his quiet air of authority and intelligence, features she seemed to have missed in their first two encounters. She wondered if it was simply the terrible pain of dealing with Lori's death and her impatience to alleviate it, for herself and for Lori's family, that blinded her to his true qualities? The sheriff had been working steadily on solving the Highview murders all the time, but unaware of that, she had thought him inactive and uncaring. Now she knew otherwise, and she felt guilty over her misjudgment.

"I just thought I'd let you know those two are safely locked up," he said, "and thanks to you, most likely they'll be put away for quite a long time."

"You deserve most of the credit, sheriff."

"Well, we won't start arguin' about that," he said, winking. "Also, your car is at Cooper's garage. They'll probably have it back to you by tomorrow in pretty good shape."

"Great. Thanks so much for all your help."

"Not at all. Thank *you* for yours. But next time, how about you just leave it to us. I hate to see young ladies ruin a good pair of shoes like you did."

Maggie grinned, and he lifted his hat to her in farewell. "We'll be in touch."

Maggie waved good-bye and watched him go out the door. His words hung in the air. Next time?

Fatigue rolled over her, now, as the last molecule of adrenaline in her weary body was used up. She slid down in the bed and pulled the covers up close to her face, closed her eyes, and let all thoughts drift away and sleep take over.

It seemed like only five minutes later that her phone rang loudly in her ear. Maggie sat up in confusion, blinking at the bright light now streaming through her window.

"Hello," she rasped as she pulled the receiver to her ear, nearly knocking the base of the phone off the table.

"Maggie! When are you coming home?" her brother, Joe, demanded, his voice piercing through her fog.

Maggie laughed, shaking the sleep from her head, and pushing the phone base safely back into place. Poor Joe. So far away, and feeling helpless and frustrated because of that. She had so much to tell him. Things that would probably earn her an earful from him, but possibly also a little respect. As his older sister, she felt she deserved that. And as her much-loved brother, he deserved something too. She sat up a little straighter to deliver it.

"Joe," she said, "you're such a nag."